Into the Fire

There's Two Sides to Every Story

C.N. Johnson

HF
PH

Happie Face Publishing House, an imprint of Happie Literacy Works, LLC

ISBN: 978-1-953181-19-0 (Paperback)

Book Cover by John Knox
Printed in the United States of America.
First printing edition, 2024.

Happie Face Publishing House
8 The Green, Suite 11313
Dover, DE 19901
business@happielitworks.com

Dedication

This book is dedicated to the loved ones that I have lost.

To my father, Rahman Zubair Johnson Sr., I proudly dedicate this book to your entrepreneurial spirit. Your unwavering hustle was truly remarkable. From cutting hair and detailing cars to opening a water ice stand, you fearlessly pursued various ventures, seeking something more. Despite returning to the regular 9-5 job to stay afloat, I know deep down you yearned for greater success, growth, and self-awareness. While I may not fully comprehend the depths of your aspirations, I am fueled by the same fire that burns within me. Rest assured, I will keep that flame ablaze and carry the torch forward.

With love, Your Daughter

C.N. JOHNSON

Also dedicated to:

Wanya Johnson

Deborah (Sonni) Hepworth

Vivian Johnson

CONTENTS

About the Chapter Playlists

Each chapter has its own playlist, so you can be in the moment, feel the mood, and envision different parts of the story. Each song will appear within the text at the moment you should play them. These songs are personally picked by me to create the experience for you.

   * Artists, writers, or producers are NOT in any way shape or form affiliated with this book.

Moving On
Sean

Chapter Playlist

- ▶ INDIA ARIE—"Healing"
- ▶ MARSHA AMBROSIUS—"Lose Myself"
- ▶ VICTORIA MONET—"On My Mama"
- ▶ MEEK MILL—"Check"

It had been almost two years since Makayla passed away. Receiving that phone call haunted my soul for months. Despite everything she had done to me and our son, her suicide affected me the most. I couldn't tell if I was hurt by a broken heart or by her selfishness. The selfishness of leaving our son motherless or the selfishness of her not taking accountability for all the pain she caused.

We ended up planning her funeral—*we* as in my sister, Twin; her husband, Joe; my friends Kelly, Mally, James, Tiff; and my amazing fiancé, Tiera, whom I call T. Makayla didn't have much family or any true friends, so for the sake of our son, we wanted to honor her properly. It wasn't anything extravagant, just a simple gathering for my son to say goodbye. Well, it was for all of us to say goodbye, really. We were saying farewell to a mother, a former lover, lost friendships, and broken hearts. In both the good times and the bad, we were all she ever really had.

I understand what you might be thinking: "But Sean, after all the cheating, lying, leaving, mistreating your son, and even the attempt to harm you by crashing her car into yours... how can you feel this way?" Our son was conceived out of love, and I will always be grateful for the gift she gave me. She wasn't a bad mother; she just didn't know how to be a good one. I wanted my son to know that I respected his mother in life *and* in death. [▶ **"Healing" by INDIA ARIE**]

About a week after Makayla's funeral, a letter came in the mail from Makayla. T and I both looked at each other apprehensively. Completely anxious, we stood silently, staring at the letter on the table for what felt like hours. With clammy hands and trembling knees, I opened the letter and sat down to read. A few sentences into reading it out loud, T suggested she give me the moment to myself and left. She felt it was something I needed to read on my own. The letter contained Makayla's last words before she took her life that night in the jail cell. It read:

Dear Sean,

If you're reading this, then my journey is now complete. Typical of me, just to up and leave, right? I guess some things never change. However, unlike before, I won't be coming back, but I'm going to give you something I never gave you before: all of me. I'm going to give you the answers to every question you ever asked. All the explanations to every clue left undiscovered. The truth about our love.

Although I may not have done a great job of showing you, I loved you with every bone in my body. I just never felt like I was on your level with anything. Even going as far back as college. When my mother died, my world ended. My sister was a druggy. Hell—she didn't truly care about me. All I had was you and Twin, but you were more focused on school, and Twin started dating Joe. Then you met all these new friends, which was so amazing for you and Twin, but I felt like I couldn't compete. My boyfriend and my best friend were living their best lives without me. So yes, I cheated on you. Not because I didn't love you, but to get you to notice me. I wanted you to notice me, Sean! But instead, you moved on. So, I came back and purposely got pregnant by you. I thought you would come with me, leave school and everything behind to be with me and the baby, but you didn't, and I don't blame you. I always felt like you were ahead of me, and that made me resent you.

I know rumors went around that I purposely ended the life of our baby because you didn't leave with me, but that was never the case. I wanted my child. I wanted that part of you. I honestly think I would have been a better mother back then. But losing your mother, your best friend, dropping out of school, and barely holding on to your boyfriend on top of being pregnant can fuck you up. So, I started drinking. Just a glass won't hurt the baby, I thought. But one led to two, and the next thing you know, I'm in tears in front of an empty bottle. When I realized what I was doing, I tried to go to bed, but once I made it up the stairs, I ended up falling back to the bottom. I was so scared to tell you the truth, thinking you would hate me for being foolish. I lied and said it was a natural miscarriage.

I never felt good enough for you. I felt like a loser. You're smart, and motivated, and all the girls wanted you because you are sexy ass fuck. All I felt that I could offer you was my body. I felt fucked up, so I acted like a fuck up. But it gets worse.

Yes, I cheated on you with Mike. Knowing that he was your best friend would surely get a reaction out of you, so I got him drunk, pushed myself on him and it happened. I knew Mike would start to feel bad about it and tell you. I knew that it would break you. I wanted you to be broken because I was broken. For some crazy reason, I thought we could be broken together. But he didn't say anything. Then months later, I found out I was pregnant and by that time things got better between us. Twin and I jumped right back into our friendship, and everything was back to how it used to be. That's when Mike wanted to tell you because he thought Lil Sean could have been his. He was right. He could have been his, but I was never going to let you find out. Things were too good for us.

So, I had Frank, a guy that my sister used to date, go and try to scare Mike into not saying anything to you. You know, just threaten him a little. That night, the one you always talk about, Mike called you and said he was coming to tell you something, but he never made it. Well, that was the night Frank and I drove to Mike's house. When Mike came out of his house, Frank walked up to him as I sat in the car. I guess Mike thought Frank was going to rob him or something because he pulled out a gun, shot Frank in the leg, and ran, but when Frank pulled his gun and shot back, he killed Mike. Things didn't go as planned; he was just supposed to scare him and threaten him to keep quiet. I jumped on the driver's side of the car, leaving Frank and Mike. I was so scared, and I couldn't tell anyone about it. I'm so, so sorry, Sean. I never meant for that to happen. I was just trying to stop anything from coming between us, but not like that. I'm glad you got a DNA test when I was gone, and I am so forever grateful our son is yours.

That secret haunted me so much it became my demon. It would be hard to face you at times. Knowing I caused the death of your best friend and that he could have been Lil Sean's father. After I had our son, the guilt got heavier—unbearable at times. Our son didn't deserve a mother like me. He deserved much more. So, I left and ran to the only person I could talk to—Frank. Being with Frank was my rush. We would get drunk, get high on coke, and, yes, sleep together. It was the only way I could escape the pain. The guilt. My demon. But the rush would soon take over my life. You were so loving, regardless of how I treated you. I became cold so you would stop loving me so much. Your love for me ate at me because I never stopped loving you. I just didn't know how to love you with this demon. I didn't know how to love my own son. I wanted to be with my son, but it seemed like a fix was a better feeling than facing reality or you, your friends, and your sister, who hated me. Even when I returned, I couldn't stay, no matter how much I wanted to. I just couldn't. [▶ **"Lose Myself" by MARSHA AMBROSIUS**]

I'm so sorry for walking out on you when Lil Sean was born and not being there for you when your mother died. I'm so sorry for hurting you repeatedly for not being able to give you the family that you always wanted.

You finally did what you should have done a long time ago. You left me. I don't blame you; I wasn't shit. But the one time I wanted to really put my all into our relationship and tell you everything, finally getting the weight off my shoulders, it was too late. My world was already dark, but now it was dark, cold, and empty. You took my son and your love away from me, and for the first time, I realized I had nothing to come back to. I lost my shit.

For months, I stared at your social media, day in and day out, watching you live the life that could have been ours with someone else. I became jealous and envious. I started drinking and snorting again. I did put my hands on Lil Sean a few times while I was using. I was so mad at you that I used to take it out on him. I'm so sorry about that.

I was completely wrong and out of my mind. I should have never put my hands on my sweet, sweet boy.

Sean, that night when I ran my car into your car, I just wanted to talk to you, cuss you out, and maybe even cause a scene, but I never meant to hurt you, and definitely not our son. I didn't even know he was in the car. I drove to your house, but as I was pulling up, I saw you hop in the car and pull off, so I followed you. You really should be more aware of your surroundings. There's crazy people out there, you know.

I followed you up until you pulled into that fancy restaurant parking lot. I figured you were meeting your girlfriend, so I pulled over and waited for you to come out. As I waited, I became anxious about how our conversation would go and even how romantic and loving you were with her. So, I reached under my seat for my liquor and started drinking. I even did a few lines. The next thing I knew, the bottle was gone, my shirt wet from tears, my eyes red. Drops of blood fell on my jeans from my nose, and there your car was, pulling out of the lot.

All I wanted to do was pull up next to you and talk to you, scream at you, cry to you, and beg for you to take me back. Never did I mean to run into you. When I pulled out of my parking spot, I meant to hit the brake to stop at the red light, but I hit the gas and ran right into you. It was truly an accident. I blacked out when I hit my head and didn't even find out that our son was in the car until I woke up in the hospital. If I weren't handcuffed to the bed, I would have taken my life right there because the thought of hurting you or our son killed me. I agreed and accepted every charge without a fight because I knew I could never undo what I did. A nice officer came up to me the next morning and told me our little guy was just fine, all because you pulled him out of the car and saved him. You're a superhero dad. Knowing that I can end these demons and be at peace, knowing my son is in the best hands in the world, and knowing you have found someone who can give you all you ever wanted makes my heart smile. I was never good for you and him. So, I'm saying goodbye. I love you both wholeheartedly until forever, my babies.

PS: There is another letter for Lil Sean. Please give it to him when he is old enough to understand. I want him to know I acknowledged my wrongs, and I was sorry for everything I put him through. Maybe one day he will forgive me.

Love,

Kay

I didn't let anyone read the letter. In fact, no one even knew I received that letter besides T. I told Twin about Frank being Mike's killer. I never told anyone how I found out or that Makayla was a part of it. I just told them I found out from the streets. Twin was able to get her DEA agent friend to help find out information on Frank. Two months later, Frank's house was raided for drugs, and they found the same gun that killed Mike. Frank was sentenced to 40 years to life for drugs and the murder of an old friend. Though it felt good to get justice for Mike, he still slept with my girlfriend at the time, so I also changed Lil Sean's middle name from Micheal to my middle name, Anthony.

T suggested I go to therapy just to have someone to talk to about all this. Of course, I passed on it. That's not something Black men do. We deal and keep it moving. For a while, I wasn't having it. But, after she and I had long conversations about the future damage this may cause Lil Sean, not to mention the damage that it could cause me, I agreed to go. I must say, it was one of the best things I could have done for myself and my son. It brought up a lot of feelings I had about my father, feelings I didn't know I had, and feelings about Makayla, to the point I didn't even think I was even in love with her. I was in love with the idea that I could be there for my family like my father wasn't. A lot of time, Black men don't seek out therapy because it's not what our culture has taught us. But I tell my brothers how much they can learn and heal from things they don't know they were going through. They don't listen to me, but maybe one day they will.

Life went on, and everything was great. Then, three months later, we were hit by more unpleasant news. T's father passed away from a heart attack, which also happened to be a few months after Frank's trial. Even though T hadn't forgiven her parents for kicking her out of the house when she was 16 and pregnant with Skylar to live with her grandmother, she still felt a deep pain inside. I was right by her side at his funeral.

When we arrived, it was uncomfortable for all of us. It was the first time I met her family, and it was also the first time Sky truly met them. They hadn't seen her since she was a baby, and it had been 17 years since T had returned to her hometown in Maryland. She had distanced herself from everyone except her grandmother, who had passed away before we met.

They say if you want to know what a woman will look like when she's older, look at her mother. I must say, Mrs. Anderson is a baddie. T is the spitting image of her if she were younger. [▶ **"On My Mama" by VICTORIA MONET**] When Mrs. Anderson saw T, she ran right to her and hugged her, her eyes watering as she touched T's belly.

"A baby?" she whispered, hugging her again. I could tell that Mrs. Anderson was overjoyed to see T, but T didn't feel the same way. I especially could tell by her fake smile and the way she said "Likewise" when her mother called her beautiful. T introduced Sky to her grandmother. Mrs. Anderson was taken aback by how old Sky was and gave her a long hug. Then T introduced me as her fiancé and the father of her babies. Mrs. Anderson was so happy to have us there. She took our hands and introduced us to other people, showing off T's ring and belly before the service.

After the service, T wanted to leave, but her mother insisted that we meet back at Tiera's childhood home for the repast. When we got to the big white house with a wraparound porch, my lord, I was mesmerized. Let's just say she didn't grow up eating "struggle meals." As much land as they had, you would think they lived deep in the South. Walking inside, I was blown away. They had sitting rooms, family rooms, dining rooms, shit—so many rooms you could get lost.

I could tell by the look on T's face that she wasn't into being back home, so I broke the ice with a joke.

"So, how many slaves lived on this land? I know a plantation when I see one," I asked.

She laughed. "No, it's not. It was my father's grandparents' house. It's been passed down throughout generations," she confirmed.

"Yeah, passed down from Masta Bill." We laughed as she hit my arm. She then looked at me with such a big smile, as if to say, "Thanks, babe, I needed that."

After about 15 minutes of walking through the house and meeting folks, Mrs. Anderson asked T to meet her in a side room. Tiera insisted I come too, so I tagged along to be her support system. Once inside, Mrs. Anderson closed the door and told us to have a seat in front of this huge desk. Mrs. Anderson sat in a huge leather office chair on the other side. It felt like we were about to do a drug deal. I coughed, uttering "cartel," and Mrs. Anderson offered to get me water.

T laughed and replied to her mother, "No, he's fine." Then she pinches my arm. Her mother goes on to apologize to her for all they had been through. She goes on to say that T's father thought being tough on her would make her stronger and more independent. T was just that. She says that she never meant for them to become so distant, but once T grew up, she pushed them away.

"You weren't there when I needed you the most—pregnancy, heartbreak, development—all the things a child needs because that's what I was. I needed support from my parents. I didn't have that." T spoke with much frustration. You could see both of their eyes start to water, but neither of them dropped a tear. I instantly felt awkward, like this was not where I wanted to be. But I sat back in the chair and held T's hand because this was where I *needed* to be—right by her side.

Mrs. Anderson moved her chair up closer to the desk and looked into T's eyes. "Baby, I'm so sorry. What we did to you was wrong. No parent is perfect. Your father believed that was the best way for you to become better than we were. We were on the edge of divorce when you got pregnant and didn't know how to handle our own issues."

T squinted her eyes. "Divorce?" she questioned.

"Yes, a divorce. We didn't want you to get caught up with what we were going through, and your father was so angry that you got pregnant at such a young age with that up-to-no-good scum bag. He knew saying anything to you about it would cause issues between you two. You and your father were both hot-heads, and so, to keep the peace, we sent you to grandmom's. We thought we were doing right by you, but everything went wrong. Your father was stuck in his way and didn't want to come to you, and you were stuck in your way and didn't want to come to us. I was stuck in the middle," she explained. "But I don't want to miss another moment. My granddaughter is a college student, and my second grandchild is on the way--"

"Second Grandchildren. They're twins," T confirmed.

"Twins!? My God," Mrs. Anderson exclaimed with great excitement. I rubbed T's belly, feeling proud of myself since I put them in her, having knocked it out of the park that night. T then placed her hand on mine. Her mother's eyes watered again as she asked us if she could be there at the birth of our children. I looked at T, and T looked at me. She glanced down at her belly and then back up at her mom.

"Of course," she said. Her mother jumped out of the chair and ran over to hug both of us. After a hearty hug, she went back to the other side of her desk and opened her desk drawer.

"Now that the hard part is over..." She took out an envelope and passed it to T. She opened it, and her eyes widened. It was a check for $150,000. My heart jumped out of my chest right before T gave back the check and denied it. I thought to myself, *Are you insane, woman?* Had she completely lost her damn mind?

"I don't want your money. All I ever wanted was you there."

Her mother took a deep breath and said, "Your pride is just that of your father's." She dropped her head then, looked up to the ceiling, laughed, and stated, "She's all you, Tom; stubborn as an ox." She grabbed T's hand, placed the check back in her hand, and said, "I never showed up for you before. Please let me show up now. I know I can never replace the pain your father and I caused you. Money won't change a thing, but let me make your wedding day one of the most special days of your life. Let me give that to you, please?"

T's eyes watered, and she agreed. As they embraced, my insides danced around with joy. Our wedding was about to be lit as fuck. [▶ "Check" by MEEK MILL] I'm still convinced Mrs. Anderson is the Godmother of Maryland, and no one can tell me anything different.

Update
Sean

Chapter Playlist

- ▶ DJ KHALED—"I Love You So Much"
- ▶ TEYANA TAYLOR—"Made It"
- ▶ LAMOGINNY—"My Year"

Fast forward a year—on July 3rd, we welcomed our two beautiful children into the world. As promised, Tiera's mother was right by her side. The twins are the perfect mix of T and me. To be honest, they are *completely* Tiera with just some of my features. They both have her face and light brown skin tone. They have my dark, curly hair and that's about it, as of now. Since we already had three names that began with "s" already—Skylar, Lil Sean, and me, Sean, Tiera wanted our children's names to begin with a T. Our beautiful 7-pound, 3-ounce baby girl was named Tayana Tiera Johnson, aka TT. Her name was easy, and we agreed right away. As for our son, coming in at a whopping 8 pounds even, it took about eight hours after he was born to finally agree. I wanted him to be named Taj, but Tiera wanted Taye. So, we asked Skylar to pick, and she agreed with Taye, but she suggested we make his middle name the same as mine and Lil Sean's, Anthony. So, we named him Taye Anthony Johnson, making his initials T.A.J. It was perfect.

The twins brought so much joy into our lives, but I must say they were a handful. I don't know how my mother did it by herself with me and Twin, but I give her all the credit. I know it couldn't be easy with one parent because even with me and T around, it is hard to keep up with them. Taj is a momma's boy. He wants all of T's attention all the time. He only wants me if she's not around. He gives people this mean mug, as if they smell, when they try to pick him up. It's as if he's saying, "Hands off me peasant!" As for my TT—she's all about her daddy unless there is food involved, then it's a free-for-all. She will turn on me in a heartbeat. She's so loveable and friendly, unlike her stuck-up brother. Her laugh is so infectious that it makes my heart melt.

Last week, they celebrated their first birthday, and it's hard to believe how quickly time has flown. Since then, they've been exploring every nook and cranny of the house, crawling and taking their first wobbly steps with excitement. Their curiosity knows no bounds, as they eagerly reach for anything in sight, often putting it in their mouths to discover new tastes and textures. It's such a joy to watch them grow and develop their little personalities as they navigate this exciting stage of their lives.

My family is growing, and I couldn't be happier, but we had to rearrange the house a bit. We put the twins in Lil Sean's old room, put Lil Sean in Sky's old room, and set up the basement like a studio for Sky. She has her very own bathroom and a cozy lounge area, making it the perfect little haven just for her. It's genuinely the best rent-free apartment anyone could ever wish for. [▶ "I Love You So Much" by DJ KHALED]

My big man, Lil Sean, is seven and just started second grade. He's doing so well. He's a dedicated gamer who spends all his time in his room focused on his games. He has friends that come over to do the same thing. He has also become a momma's boy. He doesn't do anything without talking to T first. At this point, I don't even feel like his other parent, but I love the bond that they have. It's even better for me when he asks for help with his homework—I just say go ask your mom. Sky just finished her bachelor's degree in art. We gave her a big New Orleans-style graduation party at the house and even invited her father, but that nigga didn't show. It doesn't matter anyway; I'm more than happy to take on that role. Twin got her a job at the school where she works. My big baby is an art teacher for the 5th grade. We couldn't be prouder of her. She has a little boyfriend now that comes over from time to time. He's a weird little fucker. He's this vegan hippie who only eats veggies and fruit. He wears these hammer pants with sandals every day, all day, no matter what the weather is. However, oddly enough, he only listens to old-school rap, like RUN DMC, Slick Rick, or Kurtis Blow, to name a few, but he treats her well, and that's really all that matters.

As for my crew, they are out here doing the damn thing. We are all truly living and loving life. Kelly moved to New York, got a little boyfriend, and now works as a runway director. We don't see her as much as before, but she always keeps in touch. She sends little gifts for the kids, keeping them up to date with the latest drip. She is actively pursuing and fulfilling her dreams. James is engaged to T's friend, Lay. Ever since Twin and I had that birthday party in Atlantic City four years back, they have been stuck together like shoes and leather. They just brought their first home in Allentown, where James is the new head coach of their high school football team. Tiff finally came out of the closet as a lesbian. She met this beautiful woman who also teaches at the Community College of Philadelphia. They just moved in together and got a dog. Tiff is happy now that she is living in her truth. Her growth is beautiful to see. Twin and Joe are on the same regular-degular shit. Their relationship got a little rocky since Lil Sean doesn't spend that much time at their house anymore. He was like their son they couldn't have. Joe was so used to Twin taking care of Lil Sean and staying off his back about stuff, so of course, bored ass Twin being a bullheaded Taurus, started to bump heads with Joe. They are still inseparable, though. Only death could part them. As for Mally, well, he's still him—getting cash and chasing ass. He just became the department chair of the music department at Mazetown University. It's black excellence at its best around these parts. [▶ "Made It" by TEYANA TAYLOR]

Last but not least, my irresistible fiancé, T. She is impressive. She's the best mother and partner anyone could ask for. She's all business but still always makes time for her family. She took the online training she needed to become the Regional HR Director during her maternity leave. This woman never stops working. She was promoted and is now earning a very hefty salary. She is the definition of standing on business. As for me, I recovered well from my accident. Besides my two-tone colored legs from my burns, I'm perfectly fine. I'm finally getting out of the marketing department and becoming a truck driver at Best Trucking. I will start as soon as we get back from our honeymoon. The money is not as good as T's, but we will be well off and live comfortably. I mean, with the $150,000 T's mother gave us, we didn't have to spend a dime on the wedding. In fact, we did some remodeling to the house, paid off our honeymoon, gave Sky T's old car, and T got herself a Mercedes-Benz truck, like the real boss she is. Not only that, but I walked away with $85,000 from the accident that Makayla's insurance company paid out. We took what was left over from the $150,000 and

$25,000 of my money and paid off the house. We've almost reached financial freedom, and our next goal is working towards building generational wealth. I feel like we are on the right track, and we are going to ride this train until the wheels fall off. [▶ **"My Year" by LAMOGINNY**]

THE WEDDING
Sean

Chapter Playlist

▶ EARTH, WIND & FIRE—"You and I"

▶ YO GOTTI—"F-U"

▶ KANYE WEST—"Waves"

▶ EL DeBARGE—"Someone"

▶ LUTHER VANDROSS—"So Amazing"

▶ MIGOS—"Walk It Like I Talk It"

▶ LLYOD—"Get It Shawty"

▶ NIPSEY HUSSLE—"Checc Me Out"

▶ JAZMINE SULLIVAN—"Masterpiece (Mona Lisa)"

▶ MUSIQ SOULCHILD—"Yes"

▶ MAJOR—"Why I love You"

▶ HINDA HICKS –"Our Destiny"

▶ FETTY WAP— "Trap Queen"

▶ LEE ANN WOMOCK—"I Hope You Dance"

▶ SNOH AALEGRA—"Find Someone Like You"

▶ CHLOE – "Have Mercy"

"Mrs. Johnson! I'm leaving!" I yelled up the stairs, standing at the bottom. It was the last day at work for two weeks and the big day was one day away.

"Bye babe!" she quickly yelled back.

"I don't get a kiss today?" I quipped.

She yelled back, "Saturday."

"That's a whole extra 24 hours after today. That's a long time, T. Okay, you're gonna miss my lips," I replied.

"And it's a lifetime after that, Mr. Johnson," she said as she slowly walked to the top of the steps, leaned on the wall, and smiled at me with a spit rag on her shoulder.

"More like a life sentence." I laughed hard. She threw the spit rag at me and pointed at the door, telling me to get out.

I love her so much, I thought to myself as I walked out the door and headed to work. [▶ **"You and I" by EARTH, WIND & FIRE**]

I didn't have as many vacation days as T. She took four weeks off for the wedding and honeymoon compared to my two little weeks. Today, she was bringing our babies up to the job since no one had really seen them. Plus, Big Boss Tracey was throwing her a bridal shower. Surprisingly, when I got to work, my manager had a little something for me, too. There were "congratulations" signs hung up over my desk and coffee and donuts at the front of the office. It was nice, but I just can't wait for this day to be over.

Around 12:30 p.m., T walked into my office with my babies, but not just my twins—*all* my children. Lil Sean and Sky were with her, too. I felt like a proud dad. *Damn, that's one good-looking family*, I thought to myself. There were so many "aw's," "they're so cute," and "he looks just like you." Finally, I had a family of my own. I thanked God that they were all beautiful, kind, and healthy human beings. The way my soon-to-be wife looked at me and the way my children looked up to me was a feeling that I never wanted to live without. They were my blessings on top of my blessings. [▶ **"Someone" by EL DeBarge**] In the middle of my family meet and greet, my boss got up to make an announcement.

"Can I have everyone's attention, please? As we all know, today is Sean's last day with us. Not with the company but with the department. He is now one of our truckers." Everyone clapped, but T yelled and cheered louder than the applause. I felt proud that my children were here to see me get recognized.

"And that's his soon-to-be wife back there in the back cheering him on." Everyone laughed. "We would all like to say congratulations to both of you as you embark on this journey to-gether, and we have a card up here for you. Again, congratula-tions, and please everyone, enjoy the snacks." She walked over with the card. As T walked over to me, I stood up, and we thank everyone. I took my lunch and went upstairs to the third floor for T's party they had for her in the executive conference room. Man, they had the whole conference room filled with food and gifts just for her. She really was *that* girl here. Too bad I had to go back to work and finish up my day. After about an hour of working again, Tracey gave me the ok to enjoy myself with my family and insisted that the party was for me, too.

She whispered to me, "Let someone else handle that shit. It is no longer your concern." I grabbed my little box of packed stuff from my desk and said my goodbyes. [▶ "F-U" by YO GOTTI]

The next day was all about the kids. We were going on a week-long honeymoon, so we wanted to spend some time with them before we went away. T made us breakfast while I cleaned out our above-ground pool, which we got the kids last year. That afternoon, I grilled for the family. We swam, ate, played, and chased each other around the backyard with water guns. Sky, Lil Sean, and I took our dirt bikes out for a spin, which we hadn't done in a long time. We put the twins in the pool in their floating chairs and let them glide around with their little sunglasses and sun hats on. Those two were so adorable. I wished my mom was there to see them. We had an incredible day together.

Around 6 p.m., we packed up the kids and all our stuff for the wedding and headed to the hotel. We had three suites: one for the ladies, one for the men, and one for T's mother, who would watch the kids while we enjoyed our last night before the big day. I would then get the boys in the morning to get them dressed, and T would go get TT. Until then, we were going to have some *fun*.

"Man, how you get a suite in the same hotel as your wife? Men can't be men if the ladies are around," Mally said.

"Right, Sean! I don't want Lay knocking on the door to see what we are doing," James uttered.

"T set this up. She thought it would be easier with the twins and all," I explained.

"That was cap, bro. All fucking cap," Mally laughed.

"Straight cap. She set your ass up. She knew what she was doing by locking your ass down in this hotel," James said as he opened the minibar, grabbed a drink, and plopped on the sofa.

"I hope you know you're paying for that. And nah man, it was just to make everything easier for tomorrow. She's over there doing her own thing. She's not worried about us."

"Aww, look at him sticking up for his wifey... You just love her so freaking much," Mally said, poking out his lips and making kissing noises.

"*It's to make things easier*," James and Joe both said in unison, mocking me while they all laughed.

"Aye, fuck y'all." I put up my middle finger and laughed with those assholes. "The least y'all could have done was throw a nigga a party on his last night or something. All jokes aside, that's pretty fucked up." I sensed an emotion rising within me, though I was uncertain what it was.

"No, my brother. The best man makes the plans and neither of them are here. Anyone see them?" Everyone shook their heads no.

"Twin is with the girls and unless Lil Sean bringing us some hoes, then we are fucked, my boy," James joked.

"Wow, that's crazy," I said, walking off to my room and there it was. I felt disappointed in my guys. I was in disbelief. It actually hurt my heart. *Maybe they are upset I made Twin my best woman and not them?* I thought as I unpacked my bag. Joe suggested we head over to Shakes for a few drinks, then head down to South Street and get tattoos to symbolize our brotherhood.

"Aye Sean, you good with that? Sean!" he yelled out to me after noticing I wasn't paying attention.

"Yeah, whatever," I said, walking into the bathroom to get in the shower.

"Don't get your panties in a twist, my guy. We gon' make the most of tonight." James yelled.

I threw on a pair of black fitted jeans, my Gucci shirt with the red and black snake going across the chest, my red and black Gucci sneakers, and my black MazeTown dad hat with the red and green *M* on the front. Both the shirt and sneakers were gifts from my soon-to-be wife. She said she wanted me to look good on my last night unwedded. When I asked her why, she said because she wanted me to know how much better I would look with her on my arm than by myself. As I laced up my sneakers, I couldn't help but think about how much better she made me.

"Nigga, you fucking daydreaming in here?" Mally said as he walked into my room. He tapped on the wall. "Hurry up, let's go!"

"I'm ready." I walked out into the living room. Surprisingly, James, Mally, and Joe were all wearing black.

"Y'all got a black panther meeting tonight or something? The fuck is with all the black?"

"We do all have on black, huh... we keeping up with the trend, my boy," James said, hitting my shoulder.

"Let's roll," Mally yelled, grabbing my keys and tossing them to me. We left the hotel and went to Shakes.

When I walked into Shakes, all I heard was "Surprise!"

My brothers had closed Shakes for me. So many of my homies and cousins were there, all wearing black to help me celebrate. It was an overwhelming heart-felt moment.

"Ayo, you thought we forgot about you, didn't you?" Joe yelled over the music as he rubbed my shoulder. I wiped my hands over my face. I was in shock, in aww. I thought I was going to let out a tear, but I sucked it up. I grabbed each one of my guys and gave them a hug.

"I was about to be mad with y'all dickheads. I thought y'all didn't plan shit."

"Never that, my boy, never that! We couldn't give you over to the ball and chain without having one last crazy night," Mally replied.

"Ayo, thank you! This is... This is..." I was at a loss for words. As I struggled to find them, Kelly walked up behind me and whispered in my ear.

"...This is your last night as a free man."

I turned to her, and both of our faces lit up. It had been an entire year since she moved to New York, and we hadn't gotten to see each other. She looked amazing. If I didn't know, I would have thought she was walking the runways herself instead of coordinating them. She must have been working out because her body was toned in all the right places. Arms tight, ass tight, tummy on washboard. I mean, Kel's had *really* been working out, eating right, or something. I was amazed. Don't get me wrong, she was never big or ugly. She just had that cute, chunky thickness like Lauren London in *ATL*. She wore a long, fitted black maxi dress that accentuated her curves. She also wore sandals, showing off her well-manicured toes, and a fanny pack around her waist. She had cut her hair. It was giving Halle Berry. Damn, she looked sexy as fuck. [▶ **"Waves" by KANYE WEST**]

"Hey pulchritudinous."

She laughed. "Not pulchritudinous! Boy, bye, I'm done."

I found it really funny. "Yeah, I just learned it yesterday. Can you believe that's one of Lil Sean's spelling words?" I said, and we both busted out laughing. I go in for a hug. She hugged me tightly, and I was drawn by the smell of her perfume. It must've been something foreign. It smelled rich and exotic.

"Hey, stud muffin," she said, stepping back to get another look at me. She tapped my stomach. "Are you getting a dad bod?"

"Fuck out of here, short cut," I laughed.

She played with her hair a little bit while smiling. "You like it?" she asked

"I do."

We made small talk and caught up on things. Just in talking to her, I could really see that she had changed a lot. She used to be the friend who often stirred up drama and spoke without thinking, but I noticed that she had really matured. My Kel's had embraced this new chapter in her life with grace.

"You need to come home more," I said.

"I know, I know. I'm sorry I missed the Twins' birthday, but I'm working Fashion Week this year and there were so many meetings I had to go to. Hopefully, they liked their gifts. Twin told me you have a pool now."

"Yeah, I bet. And yes, they love the floating pool seat. They were floating around in them today."

Mally walked over and handed me my drink. "Yo, sorry to break up y'alls 'shoulda, coulda, woulda' convo, but we got a party going on."

"Hi to you too, asshole," Kelly uttered.

Mally hugged and kissed Kelly on the cheek. "Hey GI Jane. You know I missed you." He said, making us laugh. Kelly struck him on the back of the head.

"You stupid! A got damn fool, you know that? And I'm not staying. I just wanted to introduce you all to my guy before I left."

"Your guy?" I questioned.

Kelly waved her guy over from the bar. Honestly, this was all new to me. I knew Kelly slept with a few guys, but I was never used to her having an actual boyfriend. I was taken aback a little. *Who was this nigga*? I was bewildered. I was so used to her just being stuck on me. It wasn't that I was jealous or anything. Maybe my ego was getting the best of me. I was feeling selfish. Like, that was *my* Kelly. She doesn't need any other dude but me. I never thought about how I would feel about her loving someone else until now. We looked at each other and smiled right before this Kevin Hart-looking ass nigga walked over. He was the same height as Kelly. Maybe 5' 7" at the most. I knew he was not hitting it like I was. Flipping her upside down and shit.

"Guys, this is my boyfriend, Kenny. Kenny, these are my boys—well, more like my brothers."

"What's up, and congratulations." Kenny stretched his hand to meet mine. I looked at it, then looked at him, and was completely annoyed by his existence. Kelly bumped my back, and I gave a half smile.

I shook his little ass baby hand and said thank you. I knew for sure he was not smacking that ass when she's throwing it back like she liked it. I used to make her call on God. He could never. Mally gave him a stare as Kelly kissed him on the cheek. She demanded that we be good and pointed to all of us.

As she walked out, she turned around and mouthed, "Be nice," to me and Mally before turning up her face and pointing at us, as if she was a mother telling her kids not to ask for anything once we got into a store. Watching her leave made me realize even more that tonight was my last night. I was about to give my all to one woman for the rest of my life. I guess Joe saw the worry on my face because he handed me a shot and said in my ear. "It really hits the night before."

"What you mean?"

"That you're never going to be with another woman. That all the single shit you did and everyone you did in your past is over. It's like all the wind has been knocked out of your body. But guess what?"

"What?"

"When you see Tiera walk down that aisle tomorrow looking beautiful, and she says her vows, pledging herself to you, all of that is going to breathe new life into you.

"You think so?"

"Brother, I know so. But until then, come on and take a good last look at these hoes.

I laughed. "Thank you," I said, before we took the shot together.

The party was everything I could have asked for; open bar, DJ, wings, and even some eye candy. Mally got these four chicks to be bottle girls and take care of all my needs for the night—drink and food needs only, that is. All my other needs were taken care of by T.

Don't worry, I'm not that type of guy.

We were all trashed when we got out of there. Shakes closed at 2 a.m., so me, the guys, and our new tag-along, Kenny, who became our designated driver, went to get tattoos. Joe, James, Mally, and I all get "MT BROTHERHOOD" on our left arms and then I decide to get my family's name tatted over my heart. Tiera, Lil Sean, Skylar, Tayana, and Taye. We didn't leave the tattoo shop until five a.m. Once we got back to the hotel, Kenny linked back up with Kels, and the guys and I crashed.

I woke up around 9:30 a.m. to a knock at the door. When I opened it, it was Twin and Tiff. Immediately they went from laughing and smiling with each other to being in shock, worried and confused.

"Oh my God. What the hell happened to you? Did you get into a fight?" Twin panicked when she noticed my tattoo bandage over my chest and arm, which also had blood on it.

"Nah, we got tatted."

"Oh, hell nah. You fools got tatted while drunk? Where is my husband? Did he get tatted too?"

"Of course, and he is in the back room on the left." I said, letting Twin and Tiff inside the room.

"Well, what did you all get? Take it off and let me see, let me see!" Tiff said, excited about the reveal.

"Well damn. You sure do love your family, don't you?" she and Twin laughed. "That's so sweet, though, bro. I'm happy for you and excited about today. I hope you don't bleed through your shirt," Twin said.

"Did all of you all get this M.T. tat? It's dope!" Tiff asked.

"We sure did."

"I got to see this shit." Twin said, taking off down the hall to Joe's room. Tiff and I walk into the kitchen area. I put some coffee on while Tiff sat at the table. There wasn't a point in going back to sleep; I was already up, and my barber was coming to cut all our hair soon. I looked over at Tiff, and she was just sitting there, smiling.

I chuckled. "What are you smiling at, crazy?"

"Awww, you're getting married, boo."

I sat next to her. "I know, right? It's crazy. Who would have thought?"

"You ready?" she asked.

"He, just better be, with all those damn names on his chest," Mally said as he woke up from sleeping on the sofa bed.

"Isn't that the damn truth," Tiff added. We laughed just as Twin and Joe walked into the kitchen.

"Come on, Tiff—let's let these drunken fools get their shit together. Sean, I'll be back with Lil Sean and Taj," Twin said as she headed for the door.

"Wait, wait, wait... How was the bachelorette party? Ya'll have strippers?" I asked.

"It was absolutely... none of your business," she said, opening the door.

"Exactly," Tiff added, prompting them both to laugh, closing the door behind them. About 15 minutes later, Twin came in with the boys, and shortly after that, the barber showed up.

Soon, things started to move very quickly. Everyone was scrambling to get dressed; we were in and out of the shower while others got their hair cut—even Twin helped me get the boys together. I went from having five hours to get ready to two hours in what seemed like five minutes. So much was happening so fast that I started getting hot. I was sweating, my heart raced, and I unknowingly paced the floor.

"Sean, you good, bro?" Mally grabbed the back of my neck.

When he said that, the whole room looked at me.

"Yeah... yeah," I replied.

"Yo, guys, I think it's time to go spin the block really quick. Suits off. Let's go," Mally said.

While in the car, Mally rolled up, James pulled out the shot glasses and liquor, and Joe pulled out the words of wisdom and encouragement. It was exactly what I needed, but it isn't *all* I need. As we pulled back up to the hotel, I sat outside and texted T:

Wifey Jawn
Today 4:15 PM

Me

> I just wanted to let you know I love you, and I can't wait to marry you, Ms. Johnson

Wifey Jawn

> Thank you, I been sitting here so nervous wondering if you were even going to show up today. Lol I

know that's crazy, but you never know. Thank you for easing my mind.

Me

You are my forever baby

Wifey Jawn

You are my forever my love

That was all I needed. I guess we were both feeling the same way because of our past relationships. Feeling uncertain about your partner's commitment can cause significant stress. I guess this is what they mean by having cold feet. *It's now show time.*

Soon, I was back upstairs with the guys; the suit was on, haircut was clean, my boys and my brothers were looking amazing, and my sister was as beautiful as ever. Casket sharp even.

The boys and I each wore cream—them with brown bow ties and me with a cream-colored one. My brothers wore brown suits with tan shirts and brown ties.

Our wedding matchup was perfect. Cody was T's man of honor. He wore the same thing as my guys, and Twin wore the bridesmaid's colors, but in a different styled dress. We quickly shuffled from the rooms to the limos, and then we were off to the vineyard. I was so nervous, but I was ready for this life-changing experience that I always dreamed of.

When we first got there, Twin took the boys to T's mom. When she came back, we sat in the limo and took a few shots to calm my nerves. Shit, *everybody* was nervous. I got emotional because my mother wasn't there with me to see me get married like she was when Twin married Joe. But Twin reassured me she would hold my hand every step of the way and be right by my side like she had always been. She was the true definition of ride-or-die.

About a half an hour after our emotional shot party, our wedding planner found us and herded us to the waiting room because the women were about to arrive. We sat in the back room just talking, joking, and laughing. The guys and Twin took another shot, but my stomach was full of nerves, so I couldn't. I had a 48-piece pack of gum that I just kept chewing.

"Alright now... keep chewing that gum and Tiera gon' be pissed that you got lock jaw tonight and can't eat that pussy," Mally said. We all laughed.

"You dumb," I chuckled, spitting the gum out. I had about three pieces left by the time the wedding planner was ready for us.

I had to have my girls, Tiff and Kelly, in my wedding. They weren't T's bridesmaids, but I wanted them to play a different role—an important role. I don't have parents or grandparents here to represent me in the front row. So, I gave that role to them.

They walked side by side down to Luther Vandross' "So Amazing." Me and Twin watched from the window, and it brought a tear to my eye. It filled my heart that two of my best friends—my sisters from another mister—were honored to step in for my mother. It was going to be an emotional day. I could feel it already.

When the DJ started playing Migos "Walk It Talk It," the groomsmen shuffled down the aisle. I know most weddings wait until the reception to come out to party songs, but I wanted to get the party started from the beginning. Why wait to get things going? Let things pop off right away. We were here to celebrate all the way through. Of course, Mally had to do his two-step dance while walking down, looking like someone's old ass grandfather. Next was Twin. She didn't want to walk down to the same song as my guys; she wanted to be all the way different, so she walked down the aisle to Lloyd's, "Get it Shawty."

Finally, it was my turn. I walked down to Nipsey Hussle's "Checc Me Out." Yo, you didn't even know how hardcore that was. In my shades, I slowly walked and bopped while lip-singing. As Cody would say, "I ate." I had the people on go, you heard me?!

Following us were the bridesmaids. The first person down the aisle was her friend from work, Becca. Following her was T's friend, Lay, then our beautiful daughter, Skylar, then Cody, and finally, my other best man and ring bearer, Lil Sean. That little dude was sharp. He asked me if he could hold the rings overnight and bring them to the wedding. He said that as the best man, he should hold them. I was nervous, but he promised me he wouldn't lose them, and he didn't. I was so proud of him. My twins came down the aisle in their white Bentley trucks, remote controlled by Cody's husband, who also threw flowers out of his jacket as he walked behind the car since we didn't have a flower girl. They all came down to Jazmine Sullivan's "Masterpiece (Mona Lisa)." Finally—the love of my life.

I was nervous, scared, happy, and excited all at once. Everyone was in place, and now it was time. The audience stood up, which prompted the camera girl to position herself in the middle of the aisle. Everyone else had their phones out, waiting for the grand reveal. I looked back at Twin. She nodded, saying, "You got this."

I nodded back, and as the beat dropped, I returned my gaze to the entryway where I would set eyes on my beautiful bride. I took a deep breath and waited for the doors to reopen.

And there she was—the most beautiful woman I've ever seen. Her long, beautiful hair was curly and flowing as she walked, and she had on a tiara that sat pretty on the top of her head. A long veil was attached to the back that dragged down the aisle behind her. She thought it was old school to wear it over her face, so she already told me ahead of time that she wasn't doing that. Her dress wasn't the normal white; it was more of a cream, like my suit, and it was strapless and backless. One thing about T, she was always going to show off her shoulders. Oh, and her boobs—my god! Those things were sitting up nice. Reminded me of her breast-feeding boobs when she had the twins. They had gotten huge. Her skin was glowing. I didn't know if she was wearing makeup or not, but her beauty was breathing the life into me that Joe spoke of. She held her sunflower bouquet in her right hand and held her mother's hand with the left.

The groomsmen and bridesmaids clapped to the beat as T walked closer. We stood face to face just as the song was ending. It was perfect. *She* was perfect. I teared up as we locked eyes, and as the pastor spoke, I couldn't stop smiling.

"We are here today to celebrate the union of Sean and Tiera. Both have prepared written vows for one another. Sean?" he said, giving me my vows. I couldn't take my eyes off her. I felt like if I opened my mouth at that moment, I was going to cry. Not just any cry—the ugly type, snotting and spitting type of cry. I had always thought men crying at their weddings was fake, just a way to make the women feel good. But now I was a believer. That shit was real. I got choked up just before I could even speak. I hit my chest and cleared my throat to pull myself together. I was determined not to cry.

"T, there are really no words that could ever be good enough to express to you the way I love you. Those words just don't exist. You deserve me! Well, I guess those words do exist," I said as I closed my letter and put it in my pocket. Everyone laughed. She laughed, flagged me off with her hand, then picked up her dress and acted like she was going to leave. "Okay, wait," I said as I pulled the letter back out to continue reading. We just laughed and smiled at each other.

"Seriously, T; I never knew love until I met you. My heart and soul weren't whole until you came into my life. I can sit here and say I am truly blessed by the man upstairs for sending you my way. You are my best friend, my partner, my teacher. The way you embraced my son as your own is the day I knew I could never live without you. You are the definition of a mother. My children are everything they are because of you. You are my backbone, my arms, my feet, my legs, my hands. And let me tell you this..." I looked at the audience.

"This woman has my back at all costs. When she thought I was outside arguing with the neighbor, she came outside in sweats and sneakers, ready for whatever was going on. John over here," I said, pointing to him, "was about to get shanked over talking about a football game." Everyone laughed. "But with all that said, I want you to always know..."

Twin handed me a mic, and I sang the chorus to Musiq Soulchild's song "Yes" loud and proud.

"Top that," I told T playfully before I handed the mic back over and everyone laughed.

The pastor handed over her vows and said, "Let him have it."

"Sean, my stubborn, hardheaded love of my life. Baby, you're one of my biggest blessings," she began, fanning her eyes with her vows to stop any tears. "This man, this man, my man." She shook her head, closed her eyes, lifted her right arm up, and waved her hand to the sky as if she were praising the Lord. People started clapping, and Kelly screamed out, "Take your time!" which had us rolling in laughter. Her bridesmaids hyped her up. She took my hands in hers.

"Baby, I am forever yours." I got choked up again. I never thought anyone besides my mother and sister could make me feel so loved. "You're a beautiful human being, inside and out. I adore the man that you are. You are strong, confident, ambitious, humble, a provider, a mentor to our children, and a leader in our household. Baby, you are my entire support system. I couldn't be more equally yoked with anyone else than I am with you."

She let go of my hands and fanned her face again. This time, Cody handed her a tissue. She laughed and thanked him. "You take your time with me. Your patience is unmatched. The first time we slept in the same bed together, I told you nothing was going to happen, and that is exactly what happened. I laid there thinking to myself, *Is he not at least going to try?*" She squinted her eyes at me. Everyone laughed.

"I was worth the try, right? I mean, come on." She put her hand on her hip and turned to the audience, modeling for them. We all agreed with her; I even put my fingers in my mouth and whistled loudly. She continued.

"But nope, you had gone right to sleep. That night, you earned my trust and respect, and every day since then, you have shown me that I was worth more than a try. You never stopped stepping up to the plate and handling your business. And some business you handled very well. Home run every time." Every woman there hyped her up even more. She smiled as I adjusted my tie, turned around to my brothers, and high-fived them while we all laughed.

"Sean, thank you for being you and loving me. I can't sing, but I know someone who can hold a tune..."

Just as she said that, someone jumped on the piano, and here came the singer, Major, walking down the aisle, singing his amazing song, *Why I Love You*. I fell apart. I mouthed to her, "How?!" She shrugged and smiled.

What a lot of people didn't know was that when T was in labor with the twins, she had a hard time. Mostly because after she gave birth, she was completely fine—until she wasn't. Besides the people in the room with us—her mother, Sky, and Twin—no one knew that she had become sick. She started vomiting, had chills, and was sweating uncontrollably. Even her heart rate and blood pressure rose. The only thing that calmed her down was me jumping into the bed with her, holding her, and singing this song to her.

As Major sang each line, I became emotional, and so did she. Forget tearing up—streams ran down my face. T wiped my face while tears still fell from hers, and it made me cry even more. I heard Twin sniffle, and when I looked over, all the bridesmaids had tissues and were dabbing their eyes. I didn't think there was a dry eye in the place. It was the most beautiful feeling I had ever experienced.

When Major finished, he shook our hands, congratulated us, and left. I needed to switch up the mood, so I got down on one knee and held T's hand up in victory over my vows. Everyone laughed and clapped. I stood up, and we wiped away each other's tears. When the pastor said I could kiss my bride, I grabbed her tightly and kissed her like never before. I could taste the beginning of great things to come. That was the moment we had all been waiting for.

"I would like to be the first to introduce this beautiful, competitive, comical couple—Mr. and Mrs. Sean and Tiera Johnson!" the pastor announced with excitement.

We turned to the crowd as they cheered. We jumped the broom, kissed again, and walked out to Hinda Hicks's song, *Our Destiny*.

After we took pictures, the real fun began. The guys and I took shots before making our entrance into the reception. Then it was just me and my wife, ready to turn this wedding out. We waited to hear the DJ scream, "Mr. and Mrs. Johnson," and strolled through the doors to Fetty Wap's *Trap Queen*, with everyone hyping us up.

We hurried to get all the wedding activities out of the way from the start so we could hit the dance floor, party, and drink all night. Shortly after eating, we cut the cake. T threw the bouquet, and then I took off her garter. Kelly's boyfriend caught the garter, and Pam from our job caught the bouquet. T danced with her mom, and when it was time for me to dance with my sister, Twin decided she wanted to give a speech first.

"Can we give a round of applause to this beautiful couple?" Everyone clapped. I knew she was about to say something funny, so I sat down in anticipation.

"You may or may not know this, but Sean and I lost our mother to cancer some years back. Although she was able to attend me and my husband's wedding, she knew that she wasn't going to make it to see her baby boy do the same. So, she left something that I've been holding on to for all these years just for this day," Twin explained before a screen appeared and a video started playing behind the DJ booth.

I looked up, and it was my mom. I got up from the table I shared with T and slowly walked over to the front, standing next to Twin. "Mommy?" I said softly to myself.

"Hi, Sean, it's Mommy... say hi, Seana."
"Hi, ugly," Twin said in the background of the video.

"She's grumpy. She didn't want me to record this, but we never know what the future has in store for us, baby. If you're watching this, it's your wedding day, because I know my wonderful daughter Seana wouldn't show this to you before then, right, Seana?"

"Yeah."

"Excuse me?"

"Yes, Mommy... but it's like you're planning to leave here."

"Hush, child."

As my sister recorded, they bickered back and forth. My mom was full of grace and resilience in her last days. She was so little and thin. By then, she was in a wheelchair. It was hard for her to eat most days because she was never hungry. I used to bring her weed to help her build an appetite, but she wouldn't smoke. She had lost a lot of her hair as well, so in the video, she wore Twin's red head wrap with the knot in the front. She loved those. She used to say, "Twin, I need one in every color." She also had on my MazeTown cardigan sweater that she adored. It fit her like a throw blanket. She would say, "It's so warm, comfy, and it smells just like my boy." I missed her so much.

"Sean, I'm so sorry I couldn't be there for you today like I was for Seana. But I always knew this day would come; that you would find a good woman to share the rest of your life with and give me lots of beautiful grandbabies. *She waves.* Hi Lil Sean! Oh, Grandma loves you so, so much! And hello to any new grandchildren I have. I also love you so, so much. While I'm not there in physical form, I am always in your heart. I'm so proud of you, my handsome boy. I know that you are doing wonderful, extraordinary things in life.

To your wife: Welcome to the family, Mrs. Johnson. You are the leading lady of the next generation of women to hold the last name Johnson. And oh, baby, this name comes with a lot. There will be days of sadness and days of pain."

"How are you going to tell her she's going to be sad and in pain on her wedding day? Sorry, lady," Twin said in the background.

"Seana, hush it up now. It's called the truth! That's what's wrong with you young girls—always wanting to sugarcoat everything, thinking marriage is a walk in the park. Now come on and stop it." We all laughed at them fussing.

"You've made me forget… oh, okay. But most importantly, there will be a lot of laughter and love. You have your work cut out for you, honey. He is stubborn, spoiled, and rotten," my mom laughed hard. "But he is patient, kind, and loyal. He's a good man. So don't you go on and hurt my boy."

T screamed, "Never!" I looked back at T, smiled, and she blew me a kiss.

"I won't hold you too long." *You can hold me up forever*, I thought to myself. "I know you have a lot of dancing and car-rying on to do. But by request, I asked the DJ to play our song and have Seana step in for my dance. I love you, baby boy.

Congratulations. Treat her right. I didn't raise no jank-ass joker of a man. I love you. Oh, and Seana, cut the rope loose. He has a wife—you took care of him long enough."

"Your son will be on his own, Mommy. He just better find a wife. I'm not taking care of his simple self," Twin said in the background.

"Thank you, Seana," my mom said rolling her eyes, annoyed with her. She blew kisses, and the tape cut off. I couldn't believe that she thought so much about my future that she would leave me a video. It was like she knew before I ever had a clue. At that moment, I just wanted to be a kid again—to run to my mommy and tell her I did it and to say, "Look, Mommy, I have a family!" I wanted her to take me into her arms like she did after school and ask me about my day. I wanted to tell her all about the kids, tell her how much I loved T, how much she really loved me, and that she was nothing like Makayla. I wanted to tell her I would never leave them like Dad left us, and that we still hadn't seen that man since he left. I wanted to tell her she would love having T as a daughter-in-law more than Joe as a son-in-law, just to make her laugh. I didn't want the tape to end. I wanted to talk back to her, not just listen to her. I wanted her to hear me.

"Mommy, please hear me. I need my mom. She should be here." Tears were falling as Twin and I looked over at each other. Then Joe came up and gave Twin my sweater—the same one my mom had on in the video. She put it on, and when she looked at me, tears were flowing from her eyes. The DJ started playing Mom's song, Lee Ann Womack's "I Hope You Dance," as Twin asked me for a dance. I nodded, but I was slowly breaking down inside. My hands started shaking, and she grabbed them and pulled me in.

"I got you," she said. I nodded again because I knew she did and always would. Joe ran back over with something else for Twin. It was a gray wig and a cane. She put the wig on, and I burst out laughing along with the rest of the room. It was the perfect bittersweet moment. We danced through the whole song, and I felt like my mom was right there watching over us. When the song ended, I hid my face in Twin's neck and bawled my eyes out—not just because of my mom, but because of my sister, who was like my second mom. I was so grateful for her. Even though it was emotional for me, I appreciated my sister for keeping this treasure hidden for so long, just for this day.

I whispered, "Thank you," in her ear right before my friends, my wife, my older kids, and even T's mom formed a circle around us. We were wrapped in a big hug full of love. Joe signaled the DJ to carry on.

It was time for me and T to have our dance together. She wiped her tears and mine, and before we had our moment, Mal handed me a shot, and we took one together. The DJ started playing our song, "Find Someone Like You" by Snoh Aalegra. I pulled myself together as my wife sang the song to me in my ear and rubbed the back of my head. At the break of the song, the DJ asked all couples to join us on the dance floor. I serenaded my wife as I stared into her eyes.

The party continued, and we were all in good spirits—no tears, just fun, laughter, and liquor. When it was time for the speeches, Cody fittingly told the story of how he hooked us up. He was short and sweet. Twin didn't say too much, but she praised my wife for being the woman she was, which brought tears to T's eyes. Naturally, that made me tear up too. Then my two oldest children gave speeches.

"Um, Mom and Dad, you guys are the best mom and dad. And um, thank you for our home, my games, food, and my room and my brother and my sisters. And um, I'm happy. Mom, you're the best mom in the whole world. Thank you for loving me," Lil Sean said before giving Sky the mic and running over to hug T and me. I could tell he was so nervous just by the way he spoke with shakiness in his voice. Everyone was in awe.

I leaned over to T and whispered, "Why is this wedding so emotional?"

She laughed and said, "I don't know," as she hugged and kissed Lil Sean all over, telling him how excellent his speech was and how much she loved it.

Next was Sky.

"Mom, Pops—I'm so glad you two found each other. I know in the beginning I wasn't really with this whole relationship, mainly because I'm very protective of my mom and her heart. She deserves the best. I needed to know what his intentions were for my mother, and he made me a promise that he has yet to break. So soon after that, my view of him quickly changed. Pops became the father I never had. The father I never even knew I needed in my life, and for that, thank you both."

T and I smiled. She was pulling on all my heartstrings.

"Thank you, Mom, for taking the time to find someone great and not just bring anyone around. Thank you, Pops, for stepping up for me whenever I needed you." I made the heart sign with my fingers and held it up. She grabbed an envelope off the table and walked to our table.

"This family means the world to me, and even though you're not my biological father, you don't need to be because what we have is just understood. So, Pops, just like my siblings and now my mother, who share the same last name..." She handed me the envelope. "...here is the official legal document that says I have changed my last name. I am now Skylar Monae Johnson."

I was in complete shock as I pulled the document from the envelope and read her full name. My mouth was stuck open. You know how in *The Grinch*, his heart grew double the size? That's how mine felt. I was beyond happy. Again, the crowd was in awe.

Once again, the floodgates holding back tears opened and drowned the room. I gave her a hug and kissed her forehead.

I said into the mic, "You already were my daughter, but I am honored for you to take my name."

The DJ said, "Y'all killing me with the tears," as he wiped his eyes. "Let's turn all the way up for this beautiful family!"

We danced for the rest of the night. We had so much fun that, at one point, we forgot we had little babies. T and I scanned the room once we realized we hadn't seen our babies. Twin noticed us and knew exactly what we were looking for.

She yelled over the music, "They are with Mrs. Anderson and Aunt Ruby!"

I gave her a kiss and told her that's why she was my best woman.

The DJ played "Nice for What" by Drake, and T did the unthinkable. She walked over to Kelly and brought her over to dance with me.

T said to Kelly, "A while ago, I stole a dance from you on this song." She put Kelly's hand into mine. "This dance belongs to you," she said, then winked.

Before she could leave, Kelly grabbed T's arm and yelled over the music, "I like a threesome." She smiled, pulling T back to dance with us.

This day was one of the best days of my life—full of tears and joy. When it was all over, we quickly changed out of our wedding clothes into regular ones. Twin took all the kids home with her in my car while T and I rushed to the airport for our flight to Fiji for our honeymoon. We took a cab because we were both torn up. I couldn't believe how much T drank. My wife was happy and feeling good.

Just as we were boarding our flight, T whispered to me, "Time to go make another baby." [▶ **"Have Mercy" by CHLOE**]

Five on Fire

Sean

Chapter Playlist

☒ SNOH AALEGRA—"Whoa"

☒ JON VINYL—"Nice Guy"

☒ DANILEIGH—"Easy"

☒ JILL SCOTT—"Whenever You're Around"

☒ VICTORIA MONET—"F.U.C.K"

☒ MESHELL NDEGEOCELLO—"Come Smoke My Herb"

☒ SAM SMITH—"Unholy"

☒ JOHN MAYER—"Gravity"

☒ SHONTELLE—"Impossible"

☒ JON REDCORN—"SiR"

☒ COCO JONES—"Double Back"

Five Years Later...

"Bae, can you hand me my towel?" T yelled from the bathroom. I got up, walked over to the bathroom, and opened the door. I handed her the towel and stood there while she dried off.

"What?" she asked.

"When you gon' shave that bush down there?"

"Boy, when I have time." She dried off her hair and looked up at me. "Is there a problem with my unwaxed bush?" She looked at me, confused.

"No, you don't let me get in that jungle, anyway. I was just asking. It's getting a little *Where the Wild Things Are,* that's all." I shrugged and walked back over to the bed to lay down. She wrapped her towel around herself and stood in the doorway with her arms crossed.

"I'm about to go on a week-long business trip to Los Angeles with a group of men tomorrow, and you're worried about why I'm not waxed?"

"Should I be worried about something else?" I asked.

"No, I'm just saying if I was all waxed and getting all fancy, that's when I think you would say something—not while I'm out here all normal," she added.

"I didn't know getting waxed was something fancy to do."

"Sean, it's late. I don't have time to entertain your mood swings. I have four kids and a demanding job, so getting waxed is far down on the list of my worries."

"Sex is last on your list, too," I mumbled under my breath.

"It's not, and you're a bad mumbler," she said as she walked to her side of the bed.

As she started to lotion herself, she stopped and turned to me. "I know I've been working a lot, but I promise when I get back, we're going to spend some time together, okay? You, me, and my bush."

We both found it amusing and laughed together.

She kissed me, finished getting dressed, grabbed her laptop, and started working.

Months passed, and we were still in the same situation—business trip after business trip. She worked nonstop and, of course, we had no sex. While T was at home, I began to get more and more frustrated with her. It often felt like work consumed her life. She would be focused on her tasks during meals, and she would take business calls on family outings, requiring everyone in the car to stay quiet. When we were in bed, she had her laptop on her lap. Meanwhile, nothing had been in my lap in about three months. Everything to T was about work. She didn't have a life outside of her job.

One night, after putting the kids to sleep, we sat in bed and watched a movie. Well, I watched the movie while she typed on her laptop. I was over it, so I moved her laptop and tried to replace it with me.

"Sean, what are you doing?" she asked as I put her laptop on the nightstand. I took off her glasses and kissed her neck.

"Come on, bae, I have to get this stuff done," she moaned. I pulled back the blankets, kissed down her chest, then lifted her shirt and started kissing her stomach.

"Bae, come on. Stop, I have to work," she said. Right as I was about to take her shorts off, she stopped me completely and shut me down. She grabbed her glasses, put them back on, and pushed me away. I thought this no-sex thing in marriage started when you were old—when I couldn't get it up, and she couldn't get wet. Shit, we were only a few years in. I was extremely sexually frustrated. *This can't be life* was all that ran through my mind.

"Bae, no, seriously, I have to get this stuff done before the morning. Give me half an hour, and I'm all yours, please? Can you do that for me?" she pleaded, poking her bottom lip out. I sighed and lay back down on my side of the bed, annoyed.

"Thank you. Thirty minutes. That's all I need, I promise."

Thirty minutes turned into five hours. I was dead asleep when she finished at three in the morning. I was on my side, facing the other way from her, so she crept up behind me and slid her hand down my pants to try to wake me up.

She whispered in my ear, "Baby, I'm done."

I was super tired, but I forced myself awake for this, just in case it wouldn't happen again for months. She started sucking on my earlobe, and right as I went to turn around, here came my cock-blocking ass twins, busting through the door, trying to sleep with us. T loved it when they came to sleep with us because she was never home, and it was the only real time she got to hold them and have them all under her. She looked back at me, almost asking for approval.

I whispered, "Fuck them kids."

She smirked and said, "Bae, stop. I can't tell them no. I never get to see them. Look how cute they are."

In my head, I thought, *Well, if you keep your ass home, you would.*

I sighed and looked at those little creatures standing in the doorway, looking like the children of the corn. I loved my kids, but right now, I wished I could karate kid-kick their asses back to their own room. I just turned around, and she allowed them to climb into bed.

She caressed my back and said, "Tomorrow." I forcefully pulled the covers back over me. I could have stayed asleep for all this. Those damn kids jumped in the bed all rough, little elbows digging into my backbone and cold-ass feet on the back of my thighs.

A week passed, and she left for another trip, but this time, it was only for a day. She was going to New York for a human resources conference and would be back at work the following day.

Maybe it's me not being understanding, I thought to myself while once again lying in bed alone.

You think she's having an affair? I asked myself. *Nah...* but just in case, I FaceTimed her. She answered the phone.

T: "Hey, bae."

Me: "You good? How's the Big Apple treating you?"

T: "Meetings were good, food not so good. Everyone went out for drinks, but I'm here trying to get through all this paperwork."

Me: "You need a day off."

T: "Babe, if I take a day off, I'll have twice the work when I come back."

Me: "Well, I'm going to order breakfast and coffee, and I'll meet you at the job so we can have a little time before I have to start work."

T: "Bae, that sounds so nice. Please say you're going to Dae's Café for my mocha peppermint caramel latte..."

Me: "Of course."

T: "That's the best news I've heard all day. Thank you, bae. I love you so much. I can't wait. I'm so sorry

I've been absent. I will make it up to you tomorrow."

Me: "That's what I like to hear. Now, get some sleep. What time does your train come?"

T: "No, sir. They arranged for a driver to get me in the morning and bring me back."

Me: "Oh, okay, Boss!"

T: "I know… Call me as soon as you get into the parking lot so I can come out and have breakfast with my fine, thoughtful husband."

Me: "Alright then, bae. I love you."

T: "I love you too. Bye." [▢ **"Whoa" by SNOH AALE-GRA**]

The next day, I got up extra early like a kid on Christmas. I got the twins to school when it opened at 5:30 a.m., ran to grab breakfast and coffee, and made it to work by 6:30 a.m. We had exactly one hour to enjoy each other's company before work. It was just a little time, but I was excited about it. I called T as soon as I pulled up, but she didn't answer. I waited five minutes and called again. She texted.

Mrs. Johnson

Today 6:39 AM

Mrs. Johnson

I'm in a meeting. I'll come out as soon as I can.

I waited. Seven o'clock came, and she still hadn't come out. I text her again.

7:05 AM

Me

> T I got to be in at 730 what's the hold up? How long is the meeting?

She never replied.

I was pissed. I waited until 7:25 a.m. before getting out of the car and heading to work. As I walked into the building, I saw her standing down the hall right before the truck yard. She saw me and put up her finger to signal me to hold up. I kept walking. I gave Brit her food and coffee, asked her to give it to T, and hopped in my truck. As I started it up, T came running toward me. I could see her start apologizing, but I just pulled off. I saw Brit hand off her stuff. Even when I tried to be the bigger person and turn a blind eye to all her shortcomings in our relationship, she still fucked shit up. I felt hopeless. ["Nice Guy" by JON VINYL]

She called, but I didn't answer. She texted, but I didn't reply. I was done being patient and giving her the benefit of the doubt. I didn't have anything to say to her.

I pulled up to my 8:30 a.m. drop-off at Miller Hill Banking. I saw the receptionist, Megan, who was always pleasant when I came in. She would even offer me coffee.

"Good morning, Sean!" she said as I walked in. I dropped her boxes off on the side of her desk.

"Morning, Meg," I said, giving her a side hug.

"Oh, you smell good today! What's that?"

"Chill, woman...I smell good everyday!"

"Man, go 'head." She hit my arm, and we laughed.

Her manager, Kris, came from the back and said, "You two are always laughing about something. Did you come to wish Megan a happy birthday?"

"Nah, you didn't tell me it was your birthday! I wouldn't have come empty-handed."

"Don't worry about it. It's just another day," she said nonchalantly, waving me off.

"Don't say that. What you getting into?"

"Nothing today, but I'm going out this weekend."

I looked at my watch. "Shit, I gotta go. Yo, what time are you going to lunch?"

"At 1:30... Why?"

"I'll be back. I'm taking you to lunch for your birthday," I said as I ran out.

"Wait," I opened the door back up. "Do you have a car? I can't drive you in my truck."

"Yeah," she laughed.

"Bet."

When I got back to the bank, she was ready to go.

"Where are we going?" she smiled.

"One of my spots. Now, are you one of those girls that's too good to eat at food chain restaurants? Like the chick on social media that was appalled by the Cheesecake Factory?"

She laughed. "No, sir."

"Ok, cool, I was just wondering. Follow me." [⧄ **"Easy" by DANILEIGH**]

I jumped back into the truck, and we headed to one of my favorite cheesesteak spots off City Line Avenue called Larry's. It was a vibe. We joked and laughed the whole time, busting it up over some steaks, fries, and wings. She told me she had never been there, even though it was only about eight minutes from her job. She liked it, though, and said she'd be back. I knew it was her birthday, but I needed this. She was a really dope person and reminded me of Kelly a bit. As we walked out, we ran into Joe, who had a look of confusion on his face, so I introduced them.

"Meg, this is my brother, Joe. Joe, this is my friend, Meg." Both of them greeted each other with a "hi."

"What brings you up this way?" I asked Joe.

"You know, Twin is starting to have cravings. Anything to make her happy."

Twin was five months pregnant. She had five miscarriages in the past. It was so painful for me to watch her go through that every time. She had two back-to-back one year. At that point, I just wanted her to stop trying. As her twin, her pain was my pain. If her heart was broken, my heart was broken. We were just that connected. There were nights that just became routine after the losses when she would come to my apartment late at night to cry. She would say she never wanted to look weak in front of Joe. As soon as she got over to my apartment, she would go sit on the couch. I would go get a pillow and the blanket off my bed, go back and sit next to her. She would always ask if Lil Sean was asleep. I would tell her yeah, then turn on the TV. I would put the pillow down, and she would lie across my lap. I'd cover her up, and she would cry. I'd sit there rubbing her head until she went to sleep. But she never gave in or gave up. She went for treatments, studied herbal remedies, and ate healthy food. The doctors were in her vagina so much that she started calling it her lab rat, which Joe hated. However, in the midst of her struggles, she still was able to finish raising me as a man and help me raise my son, Lil Sean. So, when I found out she was pregnant again, I was so happy for them. I pray that this one will make it to full term.

"I gotta go back, but thank you so much, Sean. You made my day," Meg said.

"Aww, no problem. Let me walk you to your car."

"Slide back when you're done. Imma go get my order." Joe said.

After walking Meg to her car, I walked back to meet up with Joe, who was standing outside again.

"Aye bro, what are you doing?" he asked, concerned.

"What? With her?" I pointed over to where I had just walked her to. "Bro, she's just a friend... It's her birthday, and I was just taking her out to lunch. We're not on that type of time. Trust me."

"Sean... It's me." He pointed to himself with both hands. "I know all your friends; we were all in your wedding, remember that? *Your wedding*? And given the fact you're always screaming 'no new friends,' who the hell is she? Does Tiera, your wife, know this new friend?"

"You really need to stop hanging with Twin so much. You really starting to act like a female with all the questions. I just needed to get out today clear my head and have some adult conversation. It's harmless, don't worry about it. And don't go running back to your wife saying shit. If I could hear less of my sister's mouth this year, that would be great. Brother to brother, can you do that for me?"

"All right, man, you got it. I'll leave it alone."

"Thank you." I shook his hand. "I gotta get back to work. I'll hit you up tonight," I said as I began to walk off.

"Aye bro..." Joe yells

"What's up?"

"Just be careful. Don't get caught up."

I laughed. "Never," I said and hopped back into my truck.

I got back to the yard right on time, clocked out, and headed to my car. As I walked out to the hallway, I saw T.

She approached me and asked, "Why haven't you answered your phone or texted me back?"

"I was working," I said as I passed her. She followed me out of the building.

"Stop!" she said. She ran up to me and grabbed my arm, forcing me to stop. Suddenly, a group of corporate motherfuckers walked up to talk to her.

"Hello, Tiera. Are you coming back in for the meet and greet?"

She smiled. "Yes, I'm just walking my husband to the car."

"Oh, this is the famous Mr. Johnson we hear so much about. You are one lucky guy to have this lady." He extended his hand for a handshake.

I shook his hand and said, "Yeah," then headed to my car. I heard T tell him I was just in a rush and that she would meet them inside. As I got in, she walked up to the other side of the car and knocked on the window.

"Let me in!"

I unlocked the door, and she slid in, slamming the door behind her.

"That was the CEO back there. Why were you so rude? Make yourself look bad, not me!" she said.

"I don't give a fuck who that was, Tiera! Is that what you got in the car for?"

"What is your problem?" she asked. I side-eyed her. "I understand you're upset about this morning, and I'm so sorry—I really am—but it wasn't my fault! The president and CEO of our company are in town, and you're mad at me because I have to work?"

I sat back in my seat, folded my hands, and looked at her like she was crazy.

"I don't care about all that shit, T. You're supposed to be my wife, and you're letting all this work shit come in between us."

"How, Sean? This is my job. I work like this to make the $235k a year to keep us all comfortable."

I laughed with anger as I hit the top of the steering wheel aggressively.

"Us? Shit, the only one that is comfortable is you. You're never home. I'm stuck doing every fucking thing by myself. You never have time for the kids. You're always working, even on your days off, and on top of that, I can't even get a courtesy fuck to say thank you for holding shit down. God forbid, T, you fuck me just because."

"Is that what all this is about, Sean? Sex?! You're upset because I'm not lying on my back every night so you can get on top of me? Or because I'm not home to do all the cooking, cleaning, and washing so you can feel more like a man, just because I'm the one with the successful career?"

"Get the fuck out of my car, Tiera," I said in a loud, frustrated tone.

"Excuse me?" She made a face that disapproved of my choice of words.

"I did not stutter one fucking time in that sentence. I have to pick up my kids."

She chuckled. "Your kids, huh? So, they're not my kids because I'm not there, right?"

"You said it, not me."

"You know what? You're childish." She got out, slamming the door behind her, and walked off.

I pulled up beside her and rolled down the window. "I'll make sure to tell your son that you missed his first game—the one you promised you'd be at—because you had a meet-and-greet," I said. Then I rolled up the window and drove off, leaving her standing there looking dumb.

I picked up the twins and headed to Lil Sean's first baseball game. Sean, now 12, went to school in New Jersey, where we lived. The bus picked him up and dropped him off in front of the house. I tell you, time was flying by. As a father, I was proud that my son chose to do some type of sport. But man, baseball wasn't my thing. I wished he had picked basketball so we could hoop together, but he was his own little man. He liked what he liked, and that made me even more proud of him. He did his own thing. Of course, I told him his mom couldn't make it because she had to work, that she was so sorry, and promised to be at the next game. I could tell he was a little disappointed, but he was very understanding. Plus, he was overjoyed that Sky and her boyfriend were able to come.

After the game, I took the kids to their favorite spot, The Garden. They loved pasta, and we had to celebrate—Lil Sean hit a home run. Around 7 o'clock, I got a call from T.

T: "Hey, are you guys home yet?"

Me: "Nah."

T: "Oh, okay, great. I'm going to pick up a few pizzas on my way home. Ask Lil Sean if he wants anything special, and I can grab it for him on my way."

Me: "It's cool. I took everyone to The Garden."

T: "Oh... okay, well, I guess I'll just see you all at home. How was the ga—"

I hung up before she could finish. I wasn't in the mood for T at all today. Maybe tomorrow, but not today. If she wanted to know how the game went, she should have been there. I still love her, though, so I decided to bring her home a salad. She loved the salad there.

We got back to the house just in time for baths and bedtime. I gave Taj the salad to give to his mother, and he ran it to her. Of course, when we got home, she was at the table working.

"Here, Mommy!" I heard him say from the hallway.

"For me? Aww, thank you," she said, grabbing his face and giving him a kiss. "Go take your shoes off for Mommy, please."

Lil Sean joined them in the kitchen. "Mom, you should have seen it! I hit the ball right out of the park!" he said, swinging an imaginary bat.

"No way! At your first game? And I missed it... Come here, my love." Sean walked over to her, and she gave him a hug and kissed him all over his face. "Mommy is so sorry, okay?" He nodded, showing he understood. "I'm going to make it up to you. Go take your shower so you can have some time to play your game before bed." She hugged him again.

"Okay, Mom!" He took off up the stairs.

"I'm proud of you!" she yelled from the kitchen.

"Thank you," he yelled back

"Thank you for the salad. You know it's my favorite," she said to me as I grabbed a beer from the fridge.

"Yup," I replied.

"I'm going to get the twins together tonight and then ready for school tomorrow. You don't have to worry about that, okay?"

I nodded and walked up the steps. [⏵ **"Whenever You're Around" by JILL SCOTT**]

At 4 a.m., the alarm clock went off, letting me know my wife was about to head out again on another business trip. We still hadn't spoken since our argument. But even though I was still upset inside, that was my wife, and I was always going to treat her the same, no matter what.

I followed the same routine. I got up while she got in the shower and took her bags to the front door for her. I then prepared her coffee for the ride to the airport. She liked fresh beans that had to be ground up first. I was her little personal barista. Just call me "Seanbucks." While her coffee brewed, I went back upstairs, packed her laptop and paperwork in her work bag, and brought that downstairs. When her coffee was done, I put it in her favorite tumbler and made it the way she liked it. She hated buying food at the airport, so I made her favorite avocado toast with tomato and everything bagel seasoning.

"Good morning," she said softly as she walked down the steps. I greeted her the same.

"What time will your cab get here?" I asked.

"It says five minutes," she explained. "I laid the twins' clothes out for school today. Everything is on top of their dresser."

I nodded.

"Oh, and tell Lil Sean his baseball bat is in the closet. He left it on the floor again last night. I nearly broke my neck," she added as she put her hair up into a bun.

"Okay," I replied. The conversation was very awkward this morning. I really didn't have much to say to her. Her phone dinged.

"All right, that's me." I handed her the coffee and toast. She smiled and said thank you. I walked her out the door and carried her bags to the cab. I handed over her bags to the cab driver and made sure she was in so I could close the door, but she pushed it back open.

"Are we good?" she asked.

"We're good," I replied, knowing damn well we weren't. I hadn't touched or spent time with my wife in a very long time, and this time she would be gone for three weeks, not just two, like usual. She would be out in Los Angeles, in a different time zone. We were distant, and if she couldn't see that, then I didn't know what the hell to do. She signaled me for a kiss. I ducked down into the car, kissed her, and closed the door. She mouthed "thank you," and "I love you," as the cab pulled off.

I went back in the house. I had one hour before I had to get the kids up and ready. I sat down on the sofa right before I remembered that Mally had given me an edible. I got up and reached toward the back, of the top of the fridge into my coffee can stash. I didn't want to get too high—just high enough to calm my inner self that wanted to text my wife and cuss her the fuck out—so I ate a little piece and laid on the sofa. As I scrolled through my phone, I got a text.

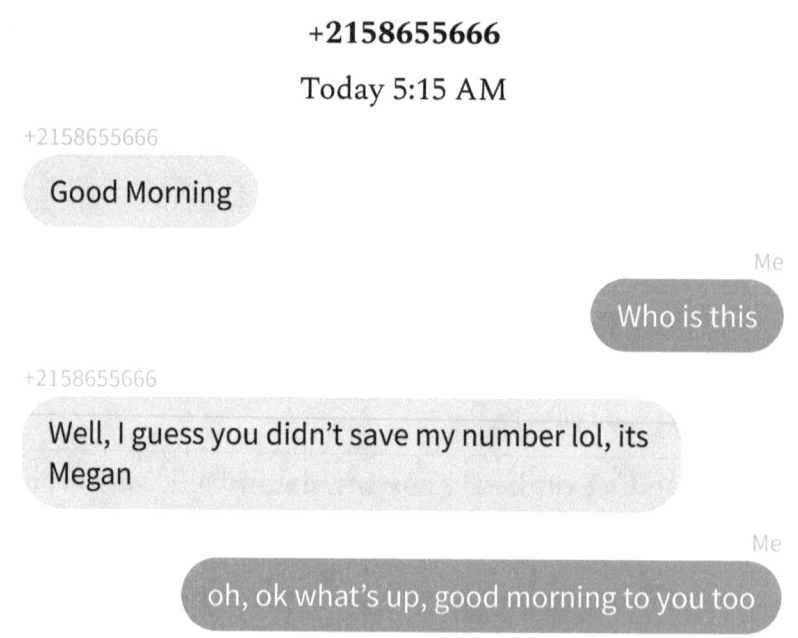

+2158655666

Today 5:15 AM

+2158655666

Good Morning

Me

Who is this

+2158655666

Well, I guess you didn't save my number lol, its Megan

Me

oh, ok what's up, good morning to you too

It started from there. Over the next week, we talked here and there. By the second week, the conversations became routine. We talked in the morning while I took the kids to school, and we had full conversations every time I dropped off packages at her office. By the third week, we were best friends. She was married as well. Her husband was in the army, and my wife was always away. We both liked to smoke to relax, we loved the same TV shows, and I found out she used to have a motorcycle, so we had a lot in common besides the fact that she didn't have any kids. We talked about everything. We laughed, joked, and built a good friendship. Nothing more than that. When T came back, we only spoke when I did my drops. Even though we were just friends, I didn't want my wife to feel like it was anything other than what it really was, and Megan understood that. It was just out of respect for T.

After a month of being home, T left again for another two weeks. Megan and I picked back up where we left off and started texting more often again. One night, while I tried to talk to T on the phone, she completely blew me off once again for work. At the same time, Megan texted me a picture of her lying in bed in a regular white tank top with no bra—I could see her nipples—and panties. This was a first. We had never sent each other photos before. So, shit, I decided to send one too.

I got up and locked the door. You already know those kids didn't care about anyone's privacy. I took off my shirt and my shorts so I could be in my underwear. I stood in front of the floor mirror and took a few pictures. I wanted to give her a full-body pic. As I looked through the pictures I took, I noticed my knees looked ashy as hell. I ran into the bathroom, got some oil, and rubbed it on my legs. Then I thought, fuck it, and rubbed some on my chest too. After going through the pictures again, I found one.

I thought about it for a moment. It was like I had the little devil on one side telling me to send it and the little angel on the other side telling me not to do it. There was a rush of excitement that came over me that I hadn't felt in a long time, so I sent it. I sat on the side of the bed and bit my thumbnail, waiting for her reply. I was scared because of my wife and the risk of this text getting out, but I was also loving the attention.

She texted back with the mouthwatering emoji. Then she told me how handsome I was, that my wife was really lucky to have me, and that she couldn't believe my wife was letting all this dick go to waste. I was flattered, so I sent her a blushing face, thanked her, and told her that her husband was missing out on a lot as well. That night, we stayed up texting until two in the morning. Whenever it got too sexual, I told her to chill. Not that I wouldn't have loved to indulge in that type of conversation, but I had already done too much with the picture. I had stepped over a line that shouldn't have been crossed. I didn't want to stop texting; I just wanted to keep it friendly. But now and then, she low-key told me all the different things she would do to my body. ["F.U.C.K" by VICTORIA MONET]

God, lead me not into temptation.

It was the week of T's return when Meg asked if I wanted to hang out. We were just friends. It was harmless, so I agreed. We planned to go to the movies tomorrow night—two days before T got back that Saturday. I called up Sky and asked her if she could watch the kids for a while. I told her I was going out, and she didn't mind. It felt good to have plans and get out of the house for a while. Day in and day out, it was just working and taking care of my kids. I felt like a housewife with a job. It felt good to have an adult conversation again. With all my friends living their own lives, Twin getting ready to have a baby of her own, nothing was the same. Sky wasn't even home half the time. She was always over at her boyfriend's house. My daily conversations consisted of Barbie dolls, who could burp the loudest, "he's not sharing," "she's not sharing," "I want," "can I have," and "I don't like." Daddy needed some adult time.

The next day, while making my run to Meg's office, we confirmed our plans. Since she lived in Delaware and I lived in Jersey, we decided to meet in the middle, in Philly. We planned to meet at the movie theater on Columbus Avenue. We decided on what we were going to see and what time to meet up. It sounded like a great plan, and I think we were both excited.

After picking the kids up, I got home around 5:30 p.m. I fed them, made sure the homework was done, and by the time I got dressed, Sky was walking through the door to take over.

"Okay, Pops, let me get a mop and a bucket for the drip you got on," Sky said, gassing me up. I had on a pair of light gray, teal, and black Yeezy Boost 700s, with black jeans, a light gray hoodie, and a silver watch and chain—nothing fancy. I hadn't really gotten dressed in a while, and I had to say, I was feeling myself as well.

"It's just a little something-something. You know how I do."

"I see you... Well, enjoy! I got these little rascals," she said, picking up TT. "And don't worry about time. I'm going to stay home tonight, and I'll take the twins to school with me in the morning."

"Aww man, you're the best." I kissed her on the forehead.

"I know. I've been telling Mom you need to start getting out more. The twins are a lot of work at times, and with Mom always working, I see how it's draining you. So, good for you—take the night off."

"Yeah, my friend from work has been trying to get me to come out for the longest, and I finally agreed. But I really miss you being here, that's on everything."

"Well, go be wild and free. I'm going to start coming home more and spending more time with you guys."

"Everything all right with you and Adam?" I asked.

"Yeah, I'm just getting bored with doing the same thing every day—work, eat, TV, and bed over and over again. I feel like I'm 40."

I laughed. "Welcome to adulthood, little baby. I love you. Thanks again."

"Love you too. Bye."

"Y'all better be good. I'm not playing," I yelled to my twins as I walked out the door.

I pulled up around 9:15 p.m. The movie started at 9:30 p.m., so I made it on time. If you had ever been to that movie theater, then you knew the parking lot was under a highway. I found a spot where there were two spaces so she could park next to me. I parked and texted Meg to let her know I was there and saving her a spot. She was down the street and pulled up five minutes later. We both exited our cars at the same time.

"Of course, you would drive a big-ass Jeep," she smiled as she walked around the car to where I was standing. "Hey, handsome, you look good in regular clothes," she said, walking in for a hug.

"I always look good; what do you mean? Even in uniform," I replied, giving her a side hug and checking her out. She wasn't Meg the Stallion, but she sure had a body. The cut of her shirt had her titties busting out, and her jeans fit just right over her ass.

"For sure, you do. So, what do you think? Do I look different from work?" she asked for confirmation as she spun around.

"Nope, head still big." We burst out laughing, and she hit my chest. "Sike, nah, you look good. Come on, let's go in before we miss the movie. Got us out here in the parking lot like it's fashion week in Paris—come on, girl," I smiled and started walking to the theater. I put my hands in my pockets just in case she thought we could be holding hands. Nope, we wouldn't be over here. I didn't want anyone seeing us and giving my wife a reason to kill me.

Once inside, we didn't even have to wait in line. Meg had already gotten our tickets. Shit, she even paid for popcorn and a few shots since the place had a bar. I didn't have to come out of my pocket at all for that outing. It couldn't have gotten any better than that. About fifteen minutes into the movie, T called. I had been trying to call her all day, and now that I was in the movies, she wanted to call—go figure. I put my phone on mute and continued to watch the movie.

After it was over and we headed back to the cars, Meg asked me if I wanted to smoke.

"Fuck yeah, I do." [◌ **"Come Smoke My Herb" by MESHELL NDEGEOCELLO**]

I hadn't had tree in a while. T didn't like it when I smoked because of the kids, so this was a treat. I had some leftover Henny in the trunk from the last time I went out with Mally so long ago. I jumped out and grabbed it. I was kid-free, didn't have to pay for anything, the movie was good, and the company was great. It was one hell of a Wednesday night.

We hopped in my car, and I drove down to a far spot in the lot where no one else was so we could chill. She handed me some tree and papers to roll up, and I handed her the bottle and two red cups. She turned on the radio while we smoked, drank, and just vibed out.

"So, you grew up in West Philly. How did you end up going to school in Cheltenham?"

"Well, my aunt Ruby lived in Cheltenham, and my mom worked at our school. So, my mom would drop us off in the morning at Aunt Ruby's house on her way to work so we could catch the bus from there to school. When she got off work, she would wait for us at Aunt Ruby's to get off the bus so no one would think anything. Then we'd drive back home to West Philly."

"Ok, Mom out here beating the system," she said.

"Yeah, she wanted us to go to better schools."

About an hour later, we were both high as a kite and a little tipsy. Meg said, "Well, I guess you better be getting back to your youngins." I looked at the time, and it was almost midnight.

"Damn, where did the time go?"

"Time always flies when you're having fun," Meg said seductively as she leaned in and kissed me. It wasn't just a tap on the lips; this was a full-blown kiss. Her tongue was down my throat. I wasn't going to lie—I was enjoying it. It had been so long. We continued to kiss as she unzipped my pants. In my head, I was screaming, *Shit! Shit! Shit! Shit!* I couldn't let this happen, so I came up with something as she went to put her hands in my pants.

"Hey, hey," I put my hands up like a gate to stop her. "I don't even have a condom to do this."

It was the best excuse I could think of at the time. Thinking that would help, she pulled my dick out and said, "You don't need it, but if you want to go further..." Then she pulled a condom box out of her bag and proceeded to give me head.

What the fuck. Did all women just carry around condoms now?

I knew at that moment I was between a rock and a hard place, but damn, it felt good as fuck. She was giving me some much-needed head. I gripped the steering wheel, trying to process what the fuck was happening. It had been so long I almost nutted in her mouth.

"Wait, wait, wait," I laughed as I pushed her off me. "I have a wife," I said, trying to catch my breath. "What are you doing?" I laid my head back on the headrest, stressed the fuck out. I was fully erect in a parking lot, cheating on my wife. I felt bad, but it felt so damn good at the same time.

She laughed. "Why so stressed out? I have a husband." She took back a shot of Henny, then poured me one. "You never got head in a parking lot before?" she asked as she handed me the shot.

"No, getting head in a parking lot is the least of my worries, woman."

"Well, he's still standing, so you can't possibly want me to stop." She said it even more seductively than before. She took another shot, bit the side of the condom wrapper, and opened it. ["Unholy" by SAM SMITH]

I got back to the house around 2:30 in the morning. I sat in the car for a while, feeling fucked up. I finally looked at my phone and saw the missed calls from T. As I scrolled, I noticed Megan had left the damn condoms on the floor. *Shit, she trying to set me up?* was the first thing that came to mind. I panicked for a second. I couldn't take them in the house. I couldn't go around back to throw them away, and we had cameras all over the outside of the house. I threw them in the glove compartment just for tonight. I'd toss them tomorrow on my way to work.

I thought everyone was asleep and I could sneak off to my room, but as soon as I opened the door, Sky yelled from the kitchen.

"Pops?"

"Yeah, it's me."

"Come here."

"Fuck," is what I was thinking, but I kept my composure and responded calmly with, "Alright."

As I came around the kitchen wall, she was at the counter talking to T on FaceTime and handed me the phone. My nerves were shot; it felt like she handed it to me in slow motion.

"Oh yeah, you had a good time. You smell just like tree and liquor, Pop," Sky laughed. *Thank God that's all she smelled.* I chuckled nervously. I got on the phone with T.

"What's up?"

Curiously, she asked, "Where you been?"

"Went to go see a movie."

"A movie? With who?" She looks at me suspiciously.

"People from work, had some drinks and smoked afterwards."

"Oh…" She paused. "Going out on a work week, huh?"

"I was asked, so I went."

"I called you like three times. Why didn't you answer?"

"I was in the movies when you called and had put my phone on mute. I just forgot to unmute it, my bad. Yo, call me on my phone. I'm about to go upstairs and give Sky back her phone." I left Sky's phone on the table and let her know where it was.

I went upstairs as T called and we continued our conversation. Sweating the whole time, I felt like I couldn't breathe until we ended the call. As I took my clothes off to hop in the shower, Meg texted me.

Co-worker M

Today 2:45AM

Co-worker M

> Thank you for a great night that was amazing. WOW!! Your wife is missing out. lol

I sighed. Not knowing what to text her back, I just hopped in the shower to gather my thoughts. I fucked up, and I fucked up *bad*. I sat in the shower and let the water run over my face. I was ashamed. *What did I just do?* [◻ **"Gravity" by JOHN MAYER**]

After my showered, I texted her:

3:15 AM

Me

> Thank you, but lines were crossed and I don't think we should speak anymore. I'm sorry Meg.

Then I blocked her number.

The next day, after work, T surprised us and came home early. Everyone was so happy she was home just in time for the weekend. No work and all play were what I prayed for.

Saturday morning, I got up early to get a full car detail. After that, since Sky was home, T and I went to the gym and then grabbed a cup of coffee—the little stuff we used to do before she started this new job. On our way home, T asked if I could stop and get her some ice cream even though we just left the gym. As I got out of the car, her phone rang. I already knew it was work.

There goes the weekend, I thought to myself.

Five On Fire, Part 2
Tiera

I knew he was upset that I had gotten a work call by the way he rolled his eyes and got out of the car. Little did he know it wasn't work but a travel agent calling about the trip I had booked for us next weekend since we had a three-day weekend.

> **Travel Agent**: "Mrs. Johnson, you're all set. Would you like your confirmation number?"
> **Me**: "Yes, give me one second while I try to find a pen."
> **Travel Agent**: "Of course."

I searched Sean's car for a pen. I opened the glove box and found a box of open condoms. My heart completely fell to the ground. I looked in the box and counted them—one was missing. I couldn't think for a second. I couldn't even feel my body.

> **Travel Agent**: "Hello...? Hello, Ma'am, are you there?"
> **Me**: "Yes... Yes, I'm sorry. I don't have a pen. Can you

send me an email?"

Travel Agent: "Of course, if you need any further assistance..."

I hung up before she could even finish. I saw Sean walking back, and I just put the condoms in my purse.

When he got back in the car, he was all happy and chipper. He handed me my ice cream and asked if I wanted to taste his flavor. But all I could do was look at him.

He laughed and asked, "What's wrong? Why are you staring at me so hard?" I was looking at him, but I wasn't really looking at him. My eyes were on him, but my head and thoughts were somewhere else.

"Sorry, nothing. My stomach just hurts, that's all," I said, before turning my head and looking out the window.

"It's probably just cramping from the workout; it had been a while," he suggested.

"Yup," I replied shortly.

Once back at the house, I walked in and grabbed a glass and a bottle of wine, then sat down at the table and poured myself a drink.

"I thought your stomach was hurting?" he asked curiously.

"Yeah, me too."

"Umm, okay, well, I'm going to take a shower." As he walked up the steps, he looked back at me. "Are you sure you're okay?" he asked.

"Yup."

"Alright..." he said and continued to walk up the steps. Soon, Sky came down, letting me know that she was about to meet up with Twin at the mall and asked me if I wanted anything.

"Mom...?" I heard what she said but forgot how to speak for a moment. I was so far out of my body right then.

"No, I'm sorry, just thinking about work."

She laughed. "Always. I'll see you later."

"Okay," I replied.

I was stuck in my head because I didn't know what to do. What if they weren't his—maybe they're one of his friends'—or what if my husband was really cheating on me? But with who? I needed answers. I heard the shower turn on, so I put my drink down, and went upstairs. I looked around the room for his phone. I couldn't find it. That was strange; he always put his wallet and phone on top of his nightstand. I searched high and low and finally found it in his pants on the floor.

I went to check it, and it asked for a password. I became anxious about what might be on his phone. In all the nine years I'd been with him, he had never had a password. I paced the floor.

"This nigga—has a password?" I said under my breath. My hands started shaking. As I sat down, my knees did too. I took a breath and tried to guess the password. Four numbers were all I needed. I tried our wedding date. Wrong. I tried his mother's birthday—nothing. As a long shot, I guessed the twins' ages and Lil Sean's age. 6612, and I was in. I scrolled and scrolled. And there it was, under "Co-worker M." Two months' worth of texts and pictures. I skimmed through, not really reading, but catching some major keywords. I sat on the bed and waited for him to get out of the shower with the phone open to their text messages next to me.

My heart jumped and skittered as I heard the water turn off. It skipped a beat as I heard the shower door open, then dropped down to my knees as his hand turned the bathroom doorknob. He walked out of the bathroom, towel around his waist and drying his hair.

"Ahhh, bae, that shower was everything, you hear me?"

"Who is she?" I asked, staring him dead in the face.

Five On Fire, Part 3
Sean

"Who is she?" T said, staring at me. For some reason, I knew right away what she was talking about, but I didn't really know how. How could she know? Then, I saw my phone on the bed. But I had a password now... Fuck, fuck, fuck! I thought, *Why didn't I just delete everything? What to say, what to say?*

"Who's who?" I replied. I didn't know if it was the steam from the bathroom or just me, but I was starting to sweat.

"Co-worker M. Meg, as you call her."

"So, you're going through my phone now?"

"Don't play with me."

"She's my friend from work."

She breathed deeply and exhaled. "You have one more time to play in my face, Sean. No one you work with, or we work with, is named Meg. Who is she?"

"I work—I mean, I deliver to her office. Just a friend I used to talk to from time to time. Noth—"

"Did you sleep with her?" she cut me off.

"Bae, I... I'm just frie—"

She stood up, walked over to me mid-sentence, and asked again, "Sean, did you sleep with her?" so softly and gently. She was so subtle that my eyes got watery because I knew what I was about to say would break her heart. But I couldn't lie to my wife.

"Ye... ummm, yes," I said, my voice cracking.

Have you ever seen that scene in *Glory* where Denzel Washington is getting whipped, and a single tear falls from his eye? Well, one single tear fell from her right eye as she stared at me. The disappointment in her eyes was world-shattering. She walked backward, held her stomach, and sat on the bed. I went over to her and dropped to my knees, apologizing over and over as she sat there, looking as if her mind was absent from her body. After about two minutes, which seemed like forever, she came to.

"Get out." I stayed on my knees, apologizing, and asked her if she could talk to me about it.

"GET THE FUCK OUT, SEAN!" she pushed me back and stood up. She paced the floor.

"LEAVE!" she yelled.

"Where do you want me to go? Please, just talk to me. I don't even have any clothes on."

"GET YOUR SHIT AND GET THE FUCK OUT!" she screamed.

"Okay! The kids," I said, grabbing clothes from my drawer.

She laughed and crossed her arms. "The kids? The same kids you weren't thinking about when you were out here screwing?" She walked over to me. "Huh, Sean? You weren't thinking about them, and you damn sure weren't thinking about me. *Me. Your wife*, Sean. I'm your fucking WIFE!" she continued to yell.

"I know, baby, I know, and I'm so sorry." I tried to grab her hand, but she pulled away from me.

"Get out."

I walked out of the room in my towel, grabbing all I could—my boxers, a shirt, and a pair of socks. As she slammed the door behind me, I looked down the hall, and all my kids were standing in front of Lil Sean's room. My twins didn't understand what was going on, so I casually told them to go play, and they ran off. But Lil Sean just stood there and gave me a look of disappointment that T had just given me. I walked down the hall, trying to talk to him, but he went into his room and closed the door before I could reach him, breaking my heart even more.

I went downstairs and put on the few clothes I'd managed to grab from the room. I didn't have any pants, my keys, or my phone, so I was stuck just sitting there. I knew I'd messed up and messed up badly. I knew she was upstairs, reading every text message. I just hoped she'd hear me out.

As I got up to get a drink from the kitchen, T came storming down the stairs, furious.

"WHY?" she demanded, rushing into the kitchen. "WHY, SEAN?" she repeated before I could get a word out, slamming her hand on the kitchen island.

I sat down on one of the bar stools, looking down. I couldn't even look at her. "I don't know."

"You don't know, huh?" she asked, her voice dripping with anger as she let out a bitter laugh. "How don't you know?"

I look at her. "T, I don't know. It just happened. It wasn't planned, it just... happened."

She rushed over to the sofa, grabbed her purse, and pulled out a box of condoms that I'd forgotten to throw away.

"It wasn't planned, huh?" She threw the box at me, hard and aggressively. "Seems like you were very prepared, my guy. Why are you lying to me right now?" she said, looking up, closing her eyes, taking a deep breath, then staring back at me.

"Yo, she brought those into the car. I thought we were just going to drink and smoke, that's it. She came on to me. She had an ulterior motive, not me."

"So, you fucked her in *your* car? In the car where *my* babies sit? The same car I just got out of? Oh, so that's why you had to get up early this morning to detail your car?" She didn't even wait for me to answer; she just nodded her head and said, "Ok, OK," reaching for the glass of wine she had poured earlier and taking a sip, still nodding and murmuring, "Umm hmm."

She set her glass down, looked me straight in the face, then picked it up again and threw the rest of her red wine in my face. I pushed my chair back and stood, wiping my face and shaking the wine off my hands.

"Are you serious?" she asked.

"No, are *you* serious?

"I understand you're upset, and you have every reason to be, but this—" I pointed to my wine-stained shirt and the mess on the floor. "This is not what we do; it's uncalled for."

"No, *this* is uncalled for." She then threw the glass at my head. I ducked just in time as the glass shattered against the cabinet. She went on, "No, *this* is uncalled for," smashing our wedding picture on the floor, then our family pictures, breaking basically every frame on our wall.

By this time, our children had started to come downstairs to see what was going on. T and I never fought like this, especially not to this extent.

"Tiera, RELAX! You're scaring the kids."

"UPSTAIRS, NOW!" she yelled at them.

"Why are you yelling at them? You're tripping."

"Oh, the same way some hoe tripped and fell on your dick?" she snapped, her tone dripping with sarcasm. "Because she's the one who had ulterior motives?" She mimicked air quotes with her hands, still speaking with biting sarcasm. "That's not the kind of thing you want your children to hear, right?"

She turned back to the kids. "UPSTAIRS, *NOW!*"

They ran up the steps as she continued wailing. "I'm sure you don't want your children to know their father is out here cheating on their mother while she's busting her ass every day for this family." She pointed her finger in my face, and yelled, "How many times did you fuck her, Sean? Since she says I'm wasting all that dick... was it a one-time thing, or is this what you do every time I leave the damn house?" She mushed me in the face.

At this point, I was starting to get irritated. She was doing way too much, and her behavior was becoming impetuous.

"FUCK IT! Yes, dad cheated. Is that what you want them to know? You know why dad cheated?"

"No, please, enlighten me." She stepped back, out of my face, and put her hand on her hip.

"Mom is never the fuck around for me or them. She's always working or traveling for work. Even when she's home, she's not home."

"So, you cheated on me because I'm working?"

"NO! I CHEATED BECAUSE YOU WEREN'T FUCKING ME, DAY AFTER FUCKING DAY, MONTH AFTER MONTH, AND NOTHING. I'M A FUCKING MAN. AIN'T NO WAY I'M MARRIED AND I'M FUCKING MY HAND MORE THAN MY WIFE. SO YES, I GOT FUCKED."

It was at that point that I *knew* I had fucked up.

Her eyes widened, and she jumped on me before I could take it back. My wife had never hit me before, but today, she didn't stop swinging. I yelled, telling her to relax, trying to get her off of me. Before I knew it, the kids were back downstairs, but now they were crying. They were telling me to stop when she was the one trying to fight me. We went from the kitchen to the living room, just tussling. She kept coming at me like a bull, and I was trying to keep her away. We were knocking things over in the living room. I fell over, blocking her hits. I think that made her even angrier because she couldn't land a punch like she wanted to. She even tried to bite me. I was seeing a side of T I had never seen before. I was slipping on the glass from the picture frames she'd smashed. My kids were still crying, asking us to stop. I kept telling her to stop for the kids.

I finally got a good hold of her and pinned her down on the sofa, holding her there. I had both of her hands pinned down.

"STOP, T!" I yelled, all out of breath.

"LET ME GO!" she yelled, but she was out of breath too, knowing that at this point, she had been defeated. I kept her down for about 10 minutes.

Just as she yelled, "Let me go!" again, Sky and Twin came running into the house. They both yelled at me to get off her. Everyone wants to blame the man, but sometimes it's not always us. I hadn't laid a hand on my wife—the whole time, she'd been trying to put hands on me.

Twin came around the sofa and yelled at me to let her go while Sky took the kids up the steps. As I let her go, T grabbed my shirt, punched me in the jaw, and kneed me in the balls. I fell to the ground. Her grip was so tight on my shirt that she nearly ripped it off my body when I fell. Twin helped me up and got in the middle of us.

"What the hell is going on?" We got a call from Lil Sean. He said you two are fighting and breaking shit... This is not like y'all." Twin said, confused.

Sky came back over and sat next to T. T got up, all out of breath, like she was the one trying to keep me off her.

"Do you want to tell them, or should I?" T asked

"Tell us what?" Sky asked.

"One of y'all needs to tell us something *now*," Twin added.

T looked at Sky and said, "Your father cheated."

Shocked, Sky replied, "Wow, Pops," and shook her head. Twin pushed me onto the sofa and said, "Really, dude? On your wife?"

"Yup. For two months, they've been texting and sending pictures every time I'm out of town on business," T said, out of breath. "And they had sex in his car."

I just sat there because they were all against me, anyway. I was the bad guy. Then T smiled, nodded, and said, "In his car." Now, the last time she did that, I wasn't ready for what was coming. This time, I was. I sat back on the sofa and braced myself. But instead of coming at me, she walked over to the door and grabbed Lil Sean's bat out of the umbrella holder. I jumped up, and like a big sister, Twin got in front of me and held her hand out.

"Now, T, I know he hurt you, but I can't let you just hurt my brother with a bat."

"Oh, I don't want him." T walked down the hall and opened the front door. All I could do was close my eyes because I knew what was about to happen.

BOW!

All I heard was glass shattering. Twin and Sky ran outside.

BOW!

More glass fell. The girls were trying to tell T to relax, but she kept talking shit and busting out my windows. By the time I reached the door, my front two car windows were gone. As she got to the back windows, the cops pulled up. I couldn't believe what was happening. I just sat on the steps in my underwear, with a busted lip and a ripped t-shirt, wine and blood staining it.

The male and female cop walked up and asked T to drop the bat.

"For what? This is my home, my driveway, and this is my cheating-ass husband's car, so this is my property." She gestured to me. "His cheating ass is over there looking idiotic. Go talk to him."

BOW!

She knocked out the backseat window.

"Ma'am, I'm not going to ask you again. Drop the bat," the cop said, putting his hand on his gun. I got up, but Twin pushed me back down.

Pregnant and all, she walked over, holding her hand out to the officers. "Wait a minute, officers, let me get the bat from her. She's not hurting anyone. This is her property, and her husband. My brother, is not worried about the car."

"She needs to drop the bat *now*," the male officer said. Twin nodded and stood in front of T. The female officer walked over to T and Twin, telling the male officer to come check on me.

As he walked over, still with his hand on his gun, he stopped and asked, "A child called and said their parents were fighting. Are you the parents they called about?"

"A child called?" I asked, confused.

"Yes, sir." He spoke

Yeah, I guess it was one of my children." He went on to ask if my children were safe and if I needed medical attention. Then I saw T's mom drive up, with Joe right behind her. What the hell? Did my kids call everyone in their contacts? I thought to myself, barely listening to what the officer was saying. I heard T's mom as she walked over to T. "Drop the bat, baby," she said calmly and pleasantly.

T turned to her mom and did precisely that. Her mother grabbed her and hugged her tightly. She whispered something in her ear, then pulled back, held her face, and told her to get in the car. T looked back at me, took off her ring, and dropped it. "I want a divorce," she said.

I jumped up and asked, "What do you mean?!" as she continued to walk away. I tried to follow her, but as soon as I started walking toward her, Joe grabbed me and pulled me back. So, I yelled out, "What you talking about, a divorce? Just like that, it's over, huh?"

Before she got in the car, she called Sky and said, "Get my kids."

"Oh, so you're gonna take my kids too?" I yelled over Joe's giant arm while Twin told me to calm down and let her go. The situation had gotten out of hand, and it was best that we be a part for now.

Frustrated, Sky walked out of the house with all the kids.

I grabbed Lil Sean's book bag as he tried to walk past me. I asked him where he was going. He looked at me and said, "I want to go with my mom."

"You want to go with your mom?" I asked, upset.

"Don't do that," Twin said to me. She removed my hand from Lil Sean's bag and told him to go ahead. "That's his mother. Don't you dare make him choose you because *you* fucked up. "You selfish dickhead." She pushed past me and walked inside the house.

I watched as T's mom pulled off, with Sky's car following behind. Next, the police left, and the neighbors went back inside. I picked T's ring up off the ground. I sat back down on the steps, still in my drawers, with a ripped-up T-shirt stained with wine and blood from my busted lip and only one sock on. I sat out there for almost an hour until Twin and Joe came back outside.

"We got up all the broken glass. I mopped too, just to make sure it was all cleaned up," Twin said.

"Thanks," I said, looking down at T's wedding ring.

Twin stood in front of me and said, "You won't look at me because you know you're dead wrong, Sean. You spent half your life trying to get Makayla to stop cheating on you, and you turn around and do it to someone who loves you unconditionally. Someone who gave you a home, a family, something you always wanted. Marriage isn't a walk in the park. It takes time and work. You're going to be tested, you're going to have bad days, but you hold on and see it through to a better day. You don't cheat. Do better, bro. I'm too pregnant for this shit," she added.

Joe patted me on the back and walked down the steps where Twin was.

"Give her a few days. She'll be back. She smashed all your shit and took the kids because she loves you, and she's angry. Now, if she would have packed a bag, left quietly, and left the ring on the table, then that would've been the end of you two." She hit my hand, and I looked up at her. "Fix it," she said, then turned and walked with Joe to the car.

I took one last look at my Jeep and went back into the house. I picked up our family picture off the sofa and lay down. My eyes watered because tomorrow was uncertain.

Five On Fire, Part 4
Tiera

It was the longest ride to my mother's house. I couldn't believe all the events that had just taken place. My children had never seen me act like that. I scared myself, so I knew they were scared. I was so out of control. When I saw my mom, I wanted to cry on her shoulder like a little girl, but as she held me, she whispered in my ear, "Don't let him see you cry." So, I didn't.

Once inside my mother's house, I wanted to get the children settled, sit down with them, and have a talk, but my mother told me to go take a long, hot bubble bath. She and Sky would tend to the kids. So that's what I did. As I looked at myself in the mirror while the bathwater was running, I could see why my mother had insisted I clean up. I had a cut on my forehead, and the blood from it had dried into a patch. My hair was a mess, and my hand was swollen from when I hit Sean. Lord have mercy, I looked like shit.

As soon as I sat in the bath, the tears started to fall. I put my hand over my mouth so no one would hear me, and I cried and cried some more. *How could he have done this to me? To our family?* I thought to myself. I whispered, "Why?" like he could hear me.

I cried, finished crying, and cried again. I put my washcloth over my mouth and screamed. I had sat there and cried so long that the water got cold. I got up, stepped out of the tub, and turned on the shower to actually clean up. But once inside, I slid down the wall to the shower floor and cried as the water ran over my face, mixing with my tears. The man I had loved for so long, the father of my children, the one who had given me his all and shared his world with me, had just broken my heart into a million little pieces. [♪ **"Impossible" by SHONTELLE**]

After three hours of sitting in the shower, my mother knocked on the door.

"Pooh Bear, can I come in?" That was the name my mother used to call me as a child because I loved that cartoon so much.

I didn't answer, but she came right in. She opened the shower door, turned off the water, took her shoes off, and sat down next to me, fully dressed.

"Today, you mourn your old relationship and whatever problems there may have been that got you two here. Tomorrow, you come up out of this. You focus on the now—that's your children—and you decide your future with your husband, whatever that may be. Crying and being sad won't change what he's done. You hurt because you loved him now, the same as you loved him yesterday. His cheating may make you look at him differently, but your heart feels the same, even with it broken. But only you can decide if your marriage is worth having or if you're better off without it. He doesn't get to dictate that anymore."

As she got up and headed toward the door, I called out to her. "Was Dad worth it?"

She looked back at me, and her voice softened. "He was worth it, but losing you wasn't worth the relationship. If I had known it would take me this long to get you back in my life, I would've let him go a long time ago."

She left and closed the door behind her. I sat there, staring into space, with tears still running down my face. So much had been going through my mind, but my mother had been right. I knew I couldn't let this hold me down or hold me back because I had children to take care of.

Once I got myself together and dressed, I went to check on my babies. Mom had them all fed and lying down in the living room, just like the old school days at Grandma's house when all the cousins used to come over. I sat at the dining room table, talking to Sky, who was being very supportive. It amazed me every day how grown up she had become. I was so very proud of her. About ten minutes later, after she had left to go back to her boyfriend's house, Lil Sean joined me at the table.

"Why are you still up, honey? Aren't you tired?" I asked him.

"Dad's been calling and texting my phone, but I'm not picking up for him."

"Yeah, he's been doing the same to my phone, but you can talk to him if you want. It's okay, my love. You don't have to stop because of me. He's still your dad."

"I know…" he said and looked down, fiddling with his fingers.

"Come here," I said, calling him over. "Do you want to talk about what happened today? I know a lot went on, and you called a lot of people," I smiled softly, "but I'm so sorry that you had to see me act like that." I pulled him into a hug.

"Oh no, Mom, I understand," he said, his voice filled with so much confidence. "Dad cheated on you."

I laughed a little, feeling a mix of pride and sadness. He was growing up and starting to understand things. He said it like, "I don't blame you, Mom."

"So, what is it?" I asked gently. He left my arms, started walking around the table, then turned to me.

"Mom? Are you still going to be my mom when you and Dad get a divorce? I mean, I know the twins and Sky will have you because you're their real mom, but I still want you to be my mom, too."

My heart broke at his words. I was so choked up, I could barely speak at first. I reached out my hand to him, pulled him in gently, grabbed his face, and looked deep into his eyes.

"I am your real mom. There is nothing fake about us. You're not a stepson to me; you're my real son, just like Taj. You can always talk to me, always count on me. Always know, without a doubt, that I am Mom. Even when you're mad at me or when you grow up and start thinking you're grown, I'll always be your mom, no matter what happens. And when you get a little girlfriend," I said with a wink, tickling him to make him laugh, "you better bring her to me first so I can check her out. And if she's not good enough for my baby, she's got to go."

He giggled, and I smiled, trying to lighten the mood.

"And I'm not thinking about divorce right now," I continued. "I want you to get all that out of your head, okay? Sometimes moms and dads fight and say things they don't mean. I'm not saying it's right, but the love we have for all of you will remain the same. Okay?"

"Okay," he said, relief in his voice.

"Go ahead and lay down." He kissed me on the cheek.

"Love you," I added softly.

"Love you too, Mom."

And as he headed off to bed, I sat for a moment, holding on to that tiny bit of peace, knowing I was still his mom no matter what.

The next day, I looked in the mirror and barely recognized myself. My eyes were puffy and red, my hair a mess, and my nose so clogged I had to keep my mouth open just to breathe. I had barely slept the night before, too exhausted from all the emotions and calls from Sean that I couldn't bring myself to pick up. I had considered turning off my phone, but I always kept it on for Sky, just in case.

When I came downstairs, there was a note on the table.

"Taking the kids out for breakfast and a little shopping spree. I figured you needed some time alone. Don't worry or wait for us. Do everything you need to do. I got them.

PS: Don't leave any more wine glasses on my table without a coaster. Love you, bye."

That lady never changed.

I had sat down on the sofa, trying to process everything that had happened, when Sky stopped by with breakfast. I was so thankful for her. She became my little grown best friend with her own money and her own sense of maturity. She was so supportive through all this, trying her best to keep my mind off everything for a while.

She asked if I was going back home anytime soon. I told her no, not yet. I hadn't been ready to face that place or him. I asked if she had been by the house, and she told me she had driven by but hadn't seen Sean's Jeep. Figures—he probably had it towed to get fixed. He couldn't do anything without that damn Jeep.

She asked if I wanted her to grab anything from the house for me or the kids. I gave her a long list. I hadn't been planning on going back anytime soon. She asked if Sean had called and if I'd spoken to him, and I showed her all the calls and texts he'd sent me.

"I'm just not ready to talk to him yet," I said. "I need to get my head right before I can have a real conversation with him."

"That's understandable," she said. "Well, I'll bring back all your stuff tonight." She kissed me on the cheek, told me she loved me, and then walked out the door.

I decided to try and rest, but my mind wouldn't stop. I had scrolled through Sean's texts and listened to his voicemails, but I still couldn't bring myself to respond.

Cheater Johnson:

Today 5:34 AM

Cheater Johnson

> Please call me when you wake up. I love you, and I'm so sorry.

6:15 AM

Cheater Johnson

> T, please answer the phone, baby, or text me back. I know you're up. Baby, talk to me.

6:45 AM

Cheater Johnson

> Baby, she meant nothing to me, bae. I swear. That's why I blocked her right after it happened. You read the texts. I told her it was a mistake. I fucked up. It will never happen again, and that's on my mama.

The morning messages had kept flooding my phone, each one more desperate than the last. The more I read, the heavier the weight of it all had pressed down on me.

7:28 AM

Cheater Johnson

> Fuck it then, Tiera. You wanna hide over at your mom's house instead of dealing with this like adults? Fine, fuck it. I guess I'm still the only one in this marriage trying to make it work.

8:45 AM

Cheater Johnson

> Bae, please, I'm sorry for talking crazy. Come home and talk to me. I need you. I need my family. I want to see my kids. Just let me explain. Baby, don't do this to me. I'm falling apart.

I could feel the tears welling up again, but I held them back. My mind had been a mess, and his words just added more chaos to it. I still couldn't bring myself to reply. I hadn't been ready to face it yet, let alone talk to him.

There had just been too much going on. On top of everything else, I had work to do, and I didn't even know when Sky would return with my laptop. The weight of it all had been overwhelming. *How could he have done this to me? How could he have betrayed our family?* I didn't have answers, but I couldn't stop the thoughts from running wild.

I had finally shut my eyes. The night's exhaustion and emotional toll were pulling me into a much-needed sleep.

I must have been truly exhausted and overwhelmed because when I woke up, it had already started getting dark outside. I must have really been out of it. Mom had come back with the kids, and Sky had dropped off our stuff.

I walked out into the living room and was greeted with abundant love from my children. They were so happy to see me and show me all the stuff Gram Gram had bought while they were out. Gram Gram loved to spoil her grandchildren even more than they already were. Sky hadn't even needed to pack and bring school clothes because Gram Gram had brought each of them a week's worth of clothes, socks, underwear—you name it, she'd brought it.

I had been truly blessed to have her back in my life and to have her be a part of my children's lives.

"Mom, all this stuff? Really?" I said to her as I walked into the kitchen. She pulled a tray of cookies out of the oven.

"What? It's just a little something to hold you guys over." She had taken off her oven mitt and pointed to a bag. "Look in there. I picked up your favorite perfume and some other things you might need."

"Aww, Mom, you shouldn't have, but I'm glad you did." I grabbed the bottle out of the bag and walked over to her to hug her. "Thank you. Thank you for everything."

"You're welcome. Oh, and Sean stopped by."

"Here? For what? What did you tell him?"

"He asked for you. I told him you were asleep to give you some time and that you'd talk to him when you're ready."

"And what did he say?"

"He said he understood and asked to see the kids. They all went outside and sat with him for a few. He talked to them a little about what was going on—nothing too serious. I was being nosy." She winked. "He brought over their tablets, and snacks, packed the twins' lunch for tomorrow, and gave Lil Sean lunch money. He really is a phenomenal dad."

"If only he could have been a phenomenal husband."

"At one point, he was. You just have to do the work to find out why he's not anymore. That's if you want to." With that, she picked up the tray of cookies and walked out of the kitchen.

Five On Fire, Part 5
Sean

I'm not going to lie, but being without my kids really made me lonely that weekend. I was used to my wife being gone, but my kids? They really were my life. I didn't know what to do without them. I spent my time cleaning their rooms, washing, and folding their clothes. Mally begged me to come over, but I was already in enough trouble, so I had to stay put.

Since my car was busted, I had to ride my motorcycle to work. I had forgotten the rush a bike gave me. I didn't usually ride it since I had three to five other passengers with me most of the time. I felt a little younger again. I figured T wasn't going to be at work, so I didn't check for her and went on about my day.

"Aye B!" I yelled through the yard. "Where's my truck?"

My truck was usually up front and one of the first to take out.

Brittany ran up, out of breath. "Hey, sorry, there's been a change."

"Fuck you mean a change, B?"

"There was a request for you to work Center City now. Your truck is on Southend, number CC87."

"This is bullshit!" I yelled. "Where the fuck is Glenn?"

"I know. That's what I said when I saw the board. But it came from higher than Glenn. He's in his office."

"You know how many stops and how much traffic there is in the city? I'm never gonna make it on time to get my kids," I said to Brittany as we walked over to Glenn's office.

"Glenn, what the—?" I said, raising my hands.

"Yeah, I know, man. It's not me, though. They're using your route for training this time."

"Charlie's route is the training route because it's the easiest."

"Not anymore, man. It's yours. I don't know who you pissed off, but people usually work their routes for 20-30 years."

After he said that, it hit me. I knew exactly who I had pissed off—my wife.

"But even though you have to deal with the traffic headache, the one-way streets, the people who just cross the street without a light, and no parking, the truckload is half your normal load, so you might get done earlier," Glenn stated.

"Alright," I said as I opened the door to leave, and B followed. As soon as Brittany got me set up in my truck all the way on the other side of the yard, I called T.

She didn't answer, so I left her a message.

"I understand you're mad at me, baby, I do. I can't express enough how sorry I am but don't fuck with my job. I got that route so I could be done on time to get the kids, and now there's no telling when I'm going to get off. Genius move. You just fucked both of us."

About 15 minutes later, I got a text from T.

World's Best Employee
Today 7:50 AM

World's Best Employee

> I'm sorry. I don't know what you're talking about. You're not on the same route you found your little bitch? Oh no… Yeah, that's tough, buddy. But our children will be fine. Thanks for your concern. Have a great day.

Motherfu—I *knew* she had something to do with it. She probably called one of her little manager friends and had it done. I couldn't even be mad; in fact, I laughed. She was really about to make my life hell. However, I was happy, she replied. It had been going on two days of her ignoring me, so I didn't expect that. I was going to take it on the chin and rock out. I made my bed, and now I had to lie in it. Maybe it was for the best, anyway; I was dreading the awkward moment of seeing Meg again after I blocked her, so this worked out.

Friday came around again, and T and the kids still hadn't come home. I spent a whole week without them; I was sick without my family. Yeah, I talked to the kids, but I wanted them home with me. I tried to talk to T, but she still wouldn't say anything to me unless it was about the kids. Even then, she just said she had it. They were fine, or she gave the phone to them. We needed to have a conversation about everything, but she just wouldn't talk to me. She even came and got her truck one day when I was at work. She had been avoiding me at all costs. [⌖ **"SiR" by JON REDCORN**]

After work, I decided to go back to Mrs. Anderson's house and try to talk to my wife. I had gotten my Jeep out of the shop, so maybe she would let me take the kids with me. But when I got there, Mrs. Anderson told me that T wasn't home. I almost didn't believe her, but T's truck wasn't there, and she invited me in. I had been over twice that week to see the kids and talk to T. I usually just stood outside, so T really must not have been there if she invited me in.

As soon as I got inside, the twins both grabbed a leg. Lil Sean was still a little upset with me; he was really taking one for the mom team, but he came and gave me a side hug and told me he loved me back after I said it. Mrs. Anderson asked if I wanted something to eat. Hell yeah, I had been eating out all week. I could go for some home-cooked food that I didn't have to make.

"Yes, ma'am," I said. She went to the kitchen and set me a place at the dining room table. I sat down, and she brought everything out to me. I was a little confused about why she was being so nice. *What did she do to this food?* My greedy butt, TT, came and asked for a piece of my steak. So, I gave her a piece to see if Mrs. Anderson would say anything, and she didn't, so I was cool. *Well, unless she was trying to take my baby out too,* I thought to myself... Nah. Mrs. Anderson sat down next to me, so I knew she was about to start talking.

"Sean, I think you are a wonderful father—absolutely amazing. Those children light up when you call them. All week, they've been asking if you're going to pick them up from school."

"Yeah, I miss my babies. I've been wanting them to come home, but T wants them to be with her."

"If you don't mind me asking, what got the best of you? I see how you are with the kids; I see how you are with my daughter. I see the strong, unconditional love you have for your family. This is not like you."

"I don't know," I said as I looked down at my plate and cut another piece of steak.

"I know a lie when I see one," she said as she took a cloth napkin and wiped the side of my face just like a mom would do. At that moment, I felt so safe and warm. I just said, "She started it," and we both laughed.

"No, really. I just missed my wife. No matter how many times I tried to talk to her about it, her work always came first. I was stressed out being a single father but married. I mean, I could go on and on, but at the end of the day, that's still no excuse for what I did. I got caught up in the moment, and I regret it every day."

"Sean, well, let me be the first to tell you. The Anderson women are very hardworking, independent women. I even see it in Skylar. We have this picture in our heads of how our lives should be, how things should go, and how we're doing this for our family. We work so hard that we tend to forget about our other responsibilities. Now, it's funny how a man could do the same thing. I'd say 80% of men spend their time building careers, only seeing their wives and children late at night, leaving the wife to take care of home, and it's okay for them. Because why? They are men. Poor women must deal with it. But let a woman do the same thing? Ha. A woman can do it all without a man, even please herself and stay loyal, but a man will always need a woman. Mr. Anderson was the same way. He cheated on me because I worked all the time. Tiera didn't know this, but he also blamed me for her getting pregnant because I wasn't around. That's why I didn't fight with him about sending her to her grandmother's house, because I blamed myself, too. Having experienced the same situation, I can see both sides of the story. Both parties are wrong here. But if you two can take both wrongs and correct them, you can make it right. I know you love Tiera and Tiera loves you; she just needs to process everything."

She took my plate, and under it, there was a piece of paper folded. I opened it, and there was an address.

I looked at Mrs. Anderson when she walked back into the dining room from the kitchen.

"Why are you still sitting here? Go get your wife," she said.

"What is she doing in the Poconos?" I asked.

"You're asking when you should be leaving," she replied.

I grabbed my stuff, gave her a kiss on the cheek, and said, "Thank you." I hugged and kissed the kids and ran out the door.

It took me almost three hours to get up there in traffic on a Friday night. Apparently, she was staying in a cabin. I had to drive up a big hill and down a long driveway just to get to it; the cabin was deep in the woods. I guess she really needed to be alone. When I finally got there, I saw two cars, one of which was T's truck, so I knew I was in the right place. I gathered myself, trying to figure out what I was going to say. It took about ten minutes for me to get out of the car. I was just so nervous about how she was going to react. I had stopped off to get her roses on my way up here, so I grabbed them from the backseat and headed to the door. I knocked twice, and T opened the door with a glass of wine in hand.

"Sean, what are you doing here?" she said, flabbergasted.

"I came to talk to you because you won't talk to me."

She shook her head, confused. "But how? Huh," she looked disoriented. "What?"

"I know, babe, just talk to me, and I'll explain everything." As I asked her to let me explain, the toilet flushed, and a guy walked out the door behind her.

"WHO THE FUCK IS THAT!" I yelled.

She rolled her eyes, pushed me out of the doorway, and stepped outside, closing the door behind her. While closing her sweater because it was cold, she said, "No one. Why are you here, Sean? How did you even know where I was? Do you have a tracker on me?"

"Nah, man, FUCK ALL THE BULLSHIT YOU'RE SAYING RIGHT NOW. ANSWER MY FUCKING QUESTION. WHO THE FUCK IS HE? I SWEAR TO GOD, TIERA!" She grabbed my hand and pulled me down the steps and over to the cars.

"Stop yelling. The owners of this cabin live in the next cabin over the hill. I don't want them to call the police."

I got in her face. "Well, you better start fucking explaining some shit, Tiera! You're up here alone, deep in the woods with some random nigga in a cabin? Tiera, are you for real?" I said, infuriated.

"So, you're driving around at work picking up random hoes to fuck in cars? That's better? I don't have to explain shit to you!" she shot back.

"Wow! That's where we are now? Yeah, I fucked up, T, and I'm so sorry, bae. I didn't want that girl; all I ever wanted was you. I felt disgusted after it happened. That's why I blocked her. I didn't want anything to do with her. I only ever wanted you, us, our family. I love you, bae. I'm *in* love with you, T. I'd been trying my hardest to talk to you for months about it, but you never fucking listen. It's always work, work, work. And now the very thing I wanted from you—time together, your love. Yet you're up here doing all that with some other nigga? If you're trying to get back at me, bae, please don't. I'm begging you. You're not this girl." I told her, getting choked up. We stared at each other for about five seconds.

"But how do I know you haven't just been doing this shit? Is that why we're not having sex? Because you're fucking this guy? Is this your side nigga?"

"Sure, Sean," she said.

"Is he all your work trips?" As what I was saying made me angrier, another car pulled up behind me. They pulled up so close that the headlights were blinding.

I was anticipating the moment to see who would get out of the car. As the doors opened, out came Lay and my sister, Twin. *What the fuck is going on here?* I thought to myself.

"Pickle head," Twin said as she bumped me, walking by with her big 7-month pregnant ass, almost making me fall.

"Hey, Sean," Lay patted me on the back as she walked past.

"The chef is here now. He said the food won't take that long. I also put another bottle of wine in the freezer, Lay. And your juice is in there too, Twin."

"Thank you!" they yell back.

"Chef?" I asked T. She smiles and turns side to side.

"Yes,"

"Not funny." We laughed. "You were about to get that man hurt."

She walked up to me and put her head on my chest, saying, "Hold me. I'm cold." So, I open my jacket, pull her inside, and wrap my arms around her.

"I didn't know you were having a girl's trip. So, I won't hold you up. But please come home when you get back. I need you. I need our kids."

"It wasn't a girl's trip. I planned this trip for *us*. I saw that my work was hurting us. I know you have been home being father and husband of the year. So, I planned a little get-away for us. I paid a chef from the area to cook all our meals, so all we had to worry about was being together. But things happened, and it was already paid for, so I called the girls out."

I looked out into the woods and continued to hold her. I watched my breath in the cold air. For a moment, I was speechless. I kissed the top of her head. The whole time, I was at home bitching because my wife was working, and here she was, planning getaways for us. Instead of just manning up, I was out here acting goofy over some attention another woman gave me. I felt stupid.

"Damn. I'm an asshole. I have been just thinking about myself. I'm sorry, babe. Thank you for doing this for us."

"Aww, that's so cute!" Twin yelled from the porch. We both laughed. "Now get in here. It's cold out here," she continued as she walked back in the cabin.

I kissed her on her forehead. "Alright, I'll see you when you get home." I let go of her, zipped up my jacket, and tried to head to my car, but she grabbed my hand.

"Stay." [🎵 **"Double Back" by COCO JONES**]

ABLAZE

Sean

Chapter Playlist

⬚ KOOL & THE GANG—"Summer Madness"

⬚ CLEO SOL—"When I'm In Your Arms"

⬚ ADELE—"Remedy"

⬚ LUCKY DAYE, MASEGO, & ALEX ISIEY—"Good & Plenty (Remix)"

⬚ H.E.R. – "Hard Place"

One month later, after the cabin trip, Joe called us from the hospital and told us that Twin was going into labor. They had to do an emergency c-section because the cord was wrapped around the baby's neck. She was only eight months along, so all of this was early. T and I dropped everything, packed the kids up, and dropped them off at T's mom's house. Once at the hospital, we waited in the waiting room. I paced the floor, asking

God to please make sure my sister and the baby were okay. She had finally been able to get to full term without losing it. She deserved to be a mom.

About an hour later, Joe came out to the waiting room. By that time, the party had grown; it was no longer just me and T. Tiff and her girlfriend, Lay and James, Mal, and of course, Sky, were all there.

"It's a girl," he said. Everyone ran up to him and jumped on him, but I knew something wasn't right. He was happy, but I could see something was wrong in his face.

"How is Twin?" I asked.

"She's fine. She wants you and T to come back."

Once back there, I grabbed my niece right out of the little hospital bassinet.

"She's so freakin' tiny and beautiful, Twin," I said.

"Yeah, she's only five pounds, two ounces," Twin replied, smiling proudly at her little girl.

"Yo, she looks just like me!" I implied.

Twin laughed. "But no, for real, she really does. It's crazy scary," Twin said. I showed her to T.

"Wow, she looks more like you than Lil Sean. She's a beauty. What's her name?" T asked.

"I know, it's scary," Twin said in total agreement.

"Her name better not be Josephine because we're changing it," I said to the new parents before turning my attention to the bundle of joy nestled in my arms. "Yes, we are. Yes, we are," I baby-talk to her. "Unk will never have you out here looking crazy," I told my niece, rocking her in my arms.

They all laughed.

"Ew, no," Twin laughed again. "Joe did try it, but her name is Jo'el," Twin said.

"So, Lil Joe. Got it." I rolled my eyes and laughed.

"Well, before we start bringing everyone back, I have to ask you two something and tell you something," Twin said as Joe walked over to her bed and held her hand.

"Okay," T and I said.

"You two, besides Joe and my baby, are the most important people in my life, and I trust you two with everything. Plus, you two, as a unit, are everything. Joe and I would like you two to be the godparents."

Our eyes lit up. Without a doubt, we both said hell yeah, no questions asked.

"You guys are the best. Now, I have to tell you something," Twin added.

The room got quiet, and I felt the mood shift. I put the baby down in the bassinet. Joe looked at Twin, and Twin looked at Joe. Then Joe tried to sneakily wipe a tear from his eye.

"What's wrong?" T asked.

"Twin, what's wrong?"

Joe spoke for her. "During the C-section, the doctors found a few masses on her uterus lining. They took a piece for a biopsy, which should take no more than 48 hours for us to get the results. It may be nothing, but there is a high chance it may be ESS—endometrial stromal sarcoma—a fast-growing, likely to spread form of uterine cancer."

After he said that, I faded out. I knew he was still talking, but I couldn't hear what he was saying. *My sister could have cancer? What? How?* I was just lost in my head.

T grabbed my hand, and I came to.

"So... so... so..." I stuttered. "What is the plan? What if it is? Why can't they get the results back to you faster? I mean, we're in a hospital, aren't we?" I became antsy.

"For right now, we're just going to pray for the best, and once we get the results, we'll take it from there," Twin said. I went over to the bed and hugged her tightly, saying, "It's going to be okay, don't worry." As I felt myself tearing up, I remembered that was the last thing she told our mom—that it would be okay—and then it wasn't. I walked out of the room.

When I left the room, I heard T say, "Let him walk it off; I'll talk to him."
T ran down the hall and caught up to me. She grabbed my arm, turned me around, and hugged me. I started to breathe heavily.

"Baby, it's going to be alright. Don't jump to conclusions so soon." I let go of her and just hung my head. She bent down and looked up at me. "Baby, it's going to be okay," she said, but in my heart, I knew it wasn't.

"She can't leave me," I told T before walking out of the hospital, leaving her standing in the hallway. Within 24 hours, we found out Twin did, in fact, have ESS. It broke all of our hearts. [🔥 **"Summer Madness" by KOOL & THE GANG**]

After two months of working on our relationship, we were back in a healthy place. Although T would never forget that I cheated on her, she had forgiven me to some degree. I didn't have a password on anything anymore—phone, tablet, laptop, nothing. Forget regular texts and phone calls. She would FaceTime me every time. She wanted to see everything. I got annoyed sometimes when she asked a hundred questions, but I knew it was my fault, and I had to bring myself back to reality. I had to win back her trust. Whatever she needed me to do to make her feel secure, that's what I'd do. [🔥 **"When I'm In Your Arms" by CLEO SOL**]

Although she still worked in her demanding field, she had become more in tune with the family. When she was home, *she was home*—no laptops or business calls. She was still gone from time to time, and you could definitely say she was always watching me, even from afar. She had my location now, and we checked in all the time. The best part was whenever she was away, we set time out to talk about our day and our problems before bed. It did wonders for us.

Not to brag, but I really put it down back at the cabin because T was two months pregnant with our fifth child. She wasn't as thrilled about it as I was. She knew that ass had to slow down with all the traveling at some point. I told her this was what happens when she let me build up; I hand out babies. I was so happy that Twin and I would both have small children who would grow up together like we did. I knew they were going to be into all kinds of things, just like we were.

Two months later, things took a turn for the worse. It was a Tuesday morning around 4:30 a.m. when I faintly heard my name being called followed by a soft cry. I got up and looked over for T, but she wasn't there. There was just blood on her side of the bed.

"T!" I yelled.

"I'm in here," she said from the bathroom.

I jumped up and ran to her. She was sitting in the tub crying, with blood everywhere. I started to panic because I didn't know what was going on.

"Baby, what's wrong? Why are you bleeding? You want me to call 911?" I got on my knees and held her as she cried.

"I think I lost the baby," she said as tears ran down her face.

"It's okay, babe, it's alright, don't cry. Come on, I got you. Let me help you up, and I'll take you to the hospital. I'm here. It's okay," I said as I lifted her out of the tub.

I started to get worried because she just kept bleeding a lot. Then she threw up and almost passed out, so I called 911 anyway. She became cold and started getting chills. I called Sky too, and luckily, she was home. She came upstairs, and then I had to calm her down before she woke up the other kids. I felt like the ambulance was taking too long, so I wrapped T up and carried her downstairs. I was going to put her in the car and take her myself, but as I was walking out the door, the ambulance pulled up and took her.

Lil Sean came running outside, asking what was wrong with Mom. I guess the lights and sirens had woken him up. I told him she was fine and had Sky take him back inside the house.

"I'll call you as soon as I know something," I told Sky.

Once at the hospital, they took her straight back. They asked me to wait in the waiting room for now. I sat there, worrying and stressing out for about an hour before the doctor came out to speak with me.

"Mr. Johnson," he called.

"Yes, that's me." I got up and walked right over to him.

"Nice to meet you," he said, shaking my hand and opening the door so we could go back. "I'm Dr. McGettigan. I'm taking over for your regular doctor, Dr. Paul. Unfortunately, she's on vacation as we didn't expect this to occur. Your wife, Tiera, has indeed suffered a miscarriage." It felt like someone hit me in the chest with a bat, but I stayed calm as we continued to talk. "I'm sorry for your loss. Since she was in her second trimester and lost a good amount of blood, we had to induce labor quickly and deliver the babies."

"Wait, so the baby is still alive? Did the baby just come early? So, it's like a preemie?"

"My apologies if I have confused you in any way. Your wife miscarried. The babies were stillborn. Since she was already 17 weeks along, the babies had formed quite a bit. They were the size of an avocado, so she had to give birth to them. It didn't take long because of the bleeding—they came right out."

When we got to the door, the doctor stopped me and said, "I'm going to give you two a few minutes, then I'll be back to discuss further."

Once in the room, I ran right to Tiera. She wrapped her arms around my neck and started to cry. "They're gone, they're both gone."

"Both? Baby, what do you mean both?" I asked, but she could barely talk.

"Twins," she said, cried harder. "I'm so sorry, baby. I'm so sorry."

"Shhhh." It didn't click in my brain until then, when the doctor kept saying babies. Damn, we had another set of twins.

"It's okay, baby. Nothing to be sorry about. It's not your fault."

I sat on the bed with her and just held her. Since I had gone through this with my sister so many times, I was able to be strong for the both of us. It hurt like hell, but I was able to stay calm for her sake. When the doctor finally came back, he spoke with us about what happened and possible reasons for the miscarriage, such as stress, Tiera's age, or a lot of other factors. There was nothing that he could pinpoint.

"The better news is that the throwing up and fainting were caused by a panic attack, so there is nothing to worry about in that area. "We're going to keep her for a few hours just to monitor her vitals. Her blood pressure and heart rate were elevated, but that's expected in a situation like this. Once they start to decrease, we will discharge her. If they haven't returned close to normal or if they've increased, we'll have to keep her overnight. She was dehydrated, so I'd also like her to finish the IV. I gave her some Tylenol for the cramping." He took a deep breath. "Now, the hard part. Tiera wanted to wait until you were in the room for you two to make the decision. Would you like to see and hold your babies?"

Tiera grabbed a few tissues, laid back on the bed, and patted her eyes.

"Keep in mind they are deceased. They are tiny and will fit in the palm of your hand. They are not fully developed, but they have arms, legs, fingers, and toes. The skin is transparent, so you will be able to see veins, bones, and things like that. Some people want to see, and some would rather not. Either way, it's perfectly fine and perfectly normal."

I looked at Tiera, and she looked at me. "Whatever you want to do, baby," I said. She looked over at the doctor and nodded her head yes.

"Ok, I will have the nurse bring them in shortly. Take all the time you need. We will discuss burial or cremation arrangements afterward. Other than that, I will check on her from time to time."

I knew we both lost our babies, but I was more heartbroken for my wife, and the fact that she was blaming herself hurt my heart even more.

"Ok, thank you," I said to the doctor.

"You're welcome, and I'm sorry this happened to you two. Please ring the button if you need anything," he said before leaving the room.

Maybe five minutes went by before they rolled in the plastic bassinet. The nurse wheeled them over to the bed. T sat up and lost it. She leaned into my chest and started crying. The hurt I felt when I saw them was something unbelievable. The way my wife cried was unbearable. I don't think I had ever felt this type of pain in my life, not even when my mother passed. I didn't feel any of this when Makayla lost our daughter back in college. Just the fact that my babies didn't even get a chance at life, a chance to be kids, grow, or play. Not even a chance to see our faces or hear our voices.

They were tiny, with reddish-purplish skin. They looked bruised, but also very, very transparent. The tips of their toes and fingers were clear. I could see their little rib cages and dark spots on their little bodies where their organs were. I could see the veins in their eyelids and all the veins running through their bodies. It was unreal. But I was glad she decided that we should say goodbye to our little boy and little girl.

The nurse asked if we wanted to hold them, and T just nodded yes. The blanket was so big for their tiny bodies. She placed our daughter in my hands and our son in T's hands. I couldn't hold it anymore—the tears came and didn't stop. We placed them both on the bed. We touched their little hands and feet. I think that hurt the most—not getting that grip when you put your finger in a baby's hand. They were cold yet super soft. I think when T saw me really let go of my emotions, she was able to hold up better. She talked to them and loved on them, and I was just a wreck. I started sobbing, snot and drool pouring from me. It was bad. She wiped my eyes and kissed my face.

"They have your ears," she said, smiling through the tears on her cheeks. Her words made me laugh despite the pain because their ears weren't fully developed yet. Her trying to lighten the load for me made me realize just how incredibly strong she was. Right then, I was broken inside.

"We should name them," she suggested.

"Yeah, I think we should, babe. What do you want to do? T's or S's or both?"

"No, something different."

"Knock, knock," the nurse said, walking in. "Are you ready, or do you need more time?"

I looked over at T, and she nodded yes. She kissed both our son and daughter and said, "Mommy and Daddy love you so much. We'll meet again." She picked them both up off the bed and handed them to me.

"Say hi to your grandma and grandpop for us and protect each other from any baby bullies up there in heaven," I said before I kissed them, making T and the nurse smile. I handed them back to the nurse, who placed them in the bassinet, covered them up, and rolled them out. We both broke down again, watching them leave.

I don't know what got into me, but I snapped. I was filled with so much anger. I stood up and began pacing the floor.

"It's not fair. What did we do to deserve this, T? We're good people. What the fuck? You got motherfuckers out here abusing their children, but yet they can keep having them back-to-back."

She grabbed my hand and pulled me back onto the bed, holding me.

She went from being fragile to being my rock. [⬜ **"Remedy" by ADELE**]

We just sat there for the next hour or so, holding each other. I even sang to her and cried with her. We talked about names and how we wanted to proceed with their deaths. After all that, we were so exhausted that we fell asleep.

We woke up two hours later. I went out into the hall to look for the doctor. I saw the nurse in the hallway.

"I'll tell the doctor you're up," she said. "He came in but didn't want to wake you two."

I thanked her and went back into the room with T.

The doctor came in shortly after.

"I didn't want to wake you, so I let you two sleep. This kind of thing can be very draining. I periodically checked your vitals, Tiera, and you're clear to go. But we'll need to know what you want your next steps to be."

T and I looked at each other, and then I spoke up.

"We would like them... Heaven and Halo... to be cremated and sent to us."

"Beautiful names," he said. "I'll get the paperwork together so you can sign, and then you'll be good to go."

We were in the hospital for 12 hours before they discharged us. T didn't speak much during the whole car ride home. Every time I looked over, I could see her wiping tears from her eyes. I just held her hand. I chose to stay strong for both of us and our children back home.

I couldn't believe my sister had gone through five of these. I couldn't even imagine the pain she must've felt over the years.

When we got home, everyone was downstairs—Sky, the kids, and my sister—well, everyone except Lil Sean. Everyone rushed to T as soon as she walked in, giving her hugs and kisses.

"Mommy's okay, mommy's okay," T kept saying softly and faintly, but I knew she wasn't.

I asked them where Lil Sean was.

"He's been in your room all morning, sitting in the chair, since before I got here. He hasn't come down. I think he was scared about T. I asked him if he wanted to eat or watch TV, and he said he just wanted to wait for his mom," Twin said.

"Yeah, I think seeing the blood really freaked him out. When you guys left, he took your bedding off, washed it, dried it, and made up the bed for you. He didn't even want any help."

"I'll talk to him," I replied.

"No," she said, putting her hand on my chest, "I'll talk to him." T walked slowly upstairs.

Twin took my hand and walked me toward the kitchen. She told TT and Taj to go play quietly in their rooms, and they ran upstairs.

"Quietly," Twin said.

Once in the kitchen, she grabbed me and hugged me, and it made me cry.

"I'm sorry you went through this so many times. It's not fair to anyone," I mumbled.

"I know. It's never fair." She pushed me back and held my arms. "You've got to be strong for these kids, for your wife, okay?" She put her hand under my chin and lifted my head. "You will get through this, you hear me? I got you, just like you had me."

I nodded and looked over to see Sky crying. I held my arm out to her. She took my hand, and I pulled her in. Twin cuddled both of us.

"We're going to get through this, all of us," Twin said, rubbing both our backs.

I pulled back and wiped my face, getting myself together. "How are you doing, by the way? Where is Jo'el?" I asked Twin.

I'm fine. It's not about me right now. It's okay to feel your emotions, Sean, and Joe has Jo'el.

"Yeah, I know… I'll be back. Imma go out back and smoke."

After about an hour and a half, I went to check on Tiera and Lil Sean because no one had come back downstairs. When I opened the door, they were both sleeping, Lil Sean wrapped in his mom's arms. They both looked so peaceful. I just walked out and closed the door.

"How are they doing?" Twin asked as soon as I came down.

"They're actually both sleeping," I said as I walked into the kitchen with her.

"Good, he probably was so afraid of losing another mother, seeing all that blood." She shook her head.

"I'm sure he was relieved when Mom walked through that door," Sky added.

"I never really thought of it like that. I'm so used to T being his mom that I forget his actual mother died."

"Well, damn," Twin said, turning around from the stove where she was cooking.

"That was cold, pops. Sheesh," Sky said.

"What? It's the truth."

"The truth or not, even though she wasn't shit, he knew Makayla was his mother, and he knows she's not here anymore. Whether he really understands her death or not, you need to check in with him from time to time. He's 12 now. He's growing up. He may have questions. Not today, but maybe a few days from now, you should have a talk with him. Just because you moved on from her doesn't mean he has."

"You're right."

"Food's done," Twin said.

Months later, Twin went in for her surgery, and it went very well. However, she would need a second surgery to remove the rest of the mass to keep the cancer from spreading. The doctor still recommended that she get on chemo, but she wouldn't do it because she was breastfeeding. I was pissed off with her at first, but my sister finally got to breastfeed her baby like she'd always wanted to. I couldn't steal that joy from her. In fact, she pumped out so much milk that they had to get a storage freezer for it. The woman was a cow, I tell you. I was so happy for her and Joe. They tried for so long, and now they had a daughter that they both adored. The way she looked up at my sister, like she knew that was her mommy and her mommy was willing to risk her life to make sure she was healthy, was priceless.

Ablaze, Part 2
Tiera

As I was leaving work, I overheard the security guard talking to a woman while I was taking my keys out of my purse.

"Sean's out on route," he told her, which got my attention. I looked up. She was a pretty young lady in her mid-30s, obviously pregnant—her belly was huge. I didn't know her, but I felt like I had seen her before.

"Oh, but here's his wife. I'm sure she could help you," he said, pointing over to me. We made eye contact. I walked over, curious to find out who she was and what she needed with Sean. Maybe I could help her, and plus, I was nosy. She told the guard never mind and walked out.

I looked at the guard; he looked at me and threw his hands up, confused. All of a sudden, chills ran down my spine, and now I had to know who she was and what she wanted with my husband. Of course, I walked out after her.

"Excuse me, excuse me," I said, fast walking behind her as she kept walking in front of me. And then it hit me. Her face. I remembered her face from the pictures in Sean's text messages. She was just a little heavier now. My God... *that's Megan*. She's the woman Sean slept with. I stopped and turned the other way, ready to run away so I wouldn't have to face her, but my head wouldn't let me do that. So, I turned back around in her direction, closed my eyes, and just yelled out, "Is it his?"

She stopped and turned around, and I could fully see the stomach she was trying to hide behind her coat. I walked up to her and asked again, motioning to her belly.

"Is it his?"

As she fixed her lips to say yes, I wanted to faint. My heart started doing backflips so fast that my watch thought I was working out. Three months after we miscarried, another woman was telling me she was about to have a baby by my husband. *Are you fucking kidding me?* And by the looks of it, it seemed like any day now.

I immediately called Sean with her standing in front of me and told him he needed to come home as soon as he got off work. I hung up and called my mother on the way home, asking her to pick up the kids from school.

"Bae, where you at?" Sean yelled as soon as he walked through the door.

I yelled back, "In the kitchen."

"What's wrong, bae?" he asked as he came around the corner into the kitchen, only to pause and look as if he had seen a ghost when he saw her sitting at our table. I invited her over because this wasn't just Sean's issue; this was our family's issue. If he was having a baby, *we* were having a baby—all three of us.

As he stood there confused, I asked him to have a seat, and the conversation began. Megan was, in fact, the woman Sean slept with when he cheated on me. Of course, there were many questions, like why she had waited so long to come forward about being pregnant. She told us that she wasn't going to say anything at first because after she told her husband she cheated, then told him she was pregnant later, he stayed and decided he was going to raise the child as their own. They had been trying for so long to conceive but couldn't. However, as her pregnancy progressed, her husband decided he couldn't raise another man's child and asked for a divorce just a month ago, when she was already six months along. Now, at seven months, she told us she wanted to let Sean know, so she tried calling him last week, but he had blocked her right after the night they slept together. So, she came to the job. She said it was up to him if he wanted to be in the child's life or not, but he didn't have to if he didn't want to.

I asked her, "Why would you ever think that was okay? Not letting Sean know you were having his child? He could have had a say in whether you should keep it or not."

She said that when she found out, there was nothing that was going to change her mind about keeping it. Nothing and no one. That was why her husband never asked her to have an abortion—because he knew nothing was going to make her get rid of it. She also said that once Sean had blocked her so quickly and never showed up at her office again, she knew I had found out about them, and she didn't want to get him in any more trouble.

Sean asked her how she knew he was the father and how that could be since he wore a condom. In my head, I felt like I was on *Family Feud*, clapping and saying, "Good answer!" She told us that Sean had been the only person she slept with while her husband was away on active duty. As for the condom, she didn't understand, but she guessed it was possible to get pregnant from that 1%.

I felt it in my heart and soul that it was his—I knew it when we made eye contact at work. However, I requested that we get a test done to make sure this was his child. She was so far along, and she agreed to make this happen. The conversation went better than I thought it would. Everyone, as in I, was very understanding. Yeah, I thought about cracking a wine bottle over her head a few times, but I kept it calm and surprisingly handled it very well.

I wanted results fast, so we made an appointment right there at the table for Sean to get swabbed the next day so we could find out as soon as possible. Before she left, I had Sean unblock her and give her my number. When it was time for her to go, I had him walk her out because he was sitting there, dumbfounded. I think he was so worried about what I thought and what I was going to do that he couldn't think for himself.

When he got back to the kitchen, we just looked at each other, and before he could start with the apologies, I stopped him, walked over to him, kissed him, and hugged him.

I told him, "Let's wait and see what the test says first before we go any further with this. If it's not yours, then we move on from this." He pulled back.

"And if it is?" he asked.

I rubbed his face, looked into his worried eyes, and whispered to him, "Fuck me. Fuck me right now."

He looked at me, confused, but said, "Yes." I took his hand and guided him upstairs. I started undressing the moment I walked into the room, completely naked by the time I reached the bed. He dropped his pants and came up behind me, kissing my neck and starting to feel on my breasts. He whispered in my ear, "Are you sure?"

"Fuck me," I said again, and he bit my neck, then bent me over on the bed. [⧉ **"Good & Plenty (Remix)" by LUCKY DAYE, MASEGO, & ALEX ISIEY**]

As soon as I felt the pressure of him inside of me, everything else just went away. At that moment, nothing else mattered—not Megan, not her child. It was just me and him. One thing about us—no matter what, we had the deepest level of intimacy. When he made love to me, he really made love to me. I mean, it was like the man created sex every time, as if it had never existed before now. He moved me up on the bed and pushed my left leg up while I laid on my stomach. He slid back inside of me, extra deep and so fulfilling in that position. He spread open my arms and interlocked his fingers with mine. Without even laying his entire body on me, he worked his lower body and stroked me slowly and deeply.

He kissed my back and whispered that he loved me in my ear. I took his hands, still interlocked with mine, and brought them close to my chest, wrapping his arms around me. I held his hands under me as he held me tight, starting to stroke harder. I didn't know what got into me, but the way he was working me out was taking me to another level. I let go of one of his hands and started sucking on his fingers. Shit, this man had just come from working all day—who knows where his hands had been, but I didn't care. Sucking his fingers was turning me on. I guess it was turning him on, too, because shortly after, he said, "Baby, I can't hold it. I'm going to come." With his fingers still in my mouth, I said, "Cum, baby. Cum deep inside of me. Please!"

When I said that, he flipped me around, still inside of me. I came before he could get me on my back. I knew it had gotten extra wet because I could see the "Oh my God" on his face when his eyes rolled back. He didn't even have to say it. Then he stroked faster and harder, his nut sack slapping against my ass, and I just kept getting wetter and wetter.

He grabbed my neck and started choking me as he came, saying, "Baby, I'm sorry. I'm so sorry, baby. I love you. I need you. I'm sorry, I'm sorry." His words started to crack as he spoke to me, and I lost it. He gave one last hard stroke as he came. I didn't know what he hit, but it went through my whole body. It made me bite his neck to the point that I couldn't let go. I squirted, and it wouldn't stop. My body went into full convulsions, and I started to cry.

He pulled out, put my legs on his shoulders, and put his face between my legs. I almost died when he started sucking up everything that was down there. I don't know what was going on that night. I always got very wet, but I had never squirted before, and I kept doing it. He loved it and had his face all in it. He had me pulling the sheets off the bed the way he was eating it. It was so good for both of us, and it only took about five minutes before he became hard again. He tried to go back inside me, but it was my turn, and I wanted to suck him silly. I made him sit on the side of the bed, and I sucked like it was a firecracker popsicle on the Fourth of July. He moaned so loudly and kept looking like he was going to pass out. Usually, when he's about to cum, he pushed me off, but this time, I pulled him close and gagged on it as he came. He slid off the bed to his knees. I swallowed and started sucking again until he begged me to stop.

When I tell you, I had him still moaning and breathing heavily, lying on his side on the floor with his eyes closed. I needed all of that at that moment. I needed to feel his love because I had been crying in silence since she showed up at our job, and it did not fail. I got up and walked over to him to help him up so we could get back to bed. Next thing you know, he was grabbing me and sitting me on his face.

"Why couldn't you just let me have this win?" I said and laughed. Then it was over for me—KO!

It took about five days to get the results back, and just like I had felt, her child was indeed his child. Forget being the adult I was when I invited her into my home. When we all had that heartfelt, grown-up conversation, all of that went out the window. It broke me when we found out. All I could think about was him doing to her what he had done to me a few days ago. Even though he may have just been in it for sex, a release, I couldn't help but think he made her feel how he made me feel. Now, the bond of a child they were about to share, on top of the fact that we had just lost our babies not too long ago, changed everything. [🔥 **"Hard Place" by H.E.R.**]

For Sean and Twin's 40th birthday, Joe and I had planned a Jamaican-themed party for them. Their gift was a vacation to Jamaica, and everyone was going—and I mean *everyone*: my mom, all the kids, the crew, and their boos. Sean didn't even know he had the week off—five days with all family and friends. I decorated everything in green, yellow, and black for the colors of the flag. Skylar had brought a bunch of fake dread-hats for the guests. Kelly's boyfriend was the bartender; I heard he made the best-mixed drinks. I had his bar hut set up outside. He said he'd made a signature drink for both Sean and Twin. Kelly said he was so excited to be included. Lil Sean made a playlist on his tablet, so I guess you could say he was the DJ. I didn't usually allow it because of the kids, but I had brought this enclosed blow-up so the adults could go in there and smoke. Joe and I had gone half on two ounces of weed. I had arranged for the private chef, Ryan, who joined us on the cabin trip, to prepare Caribbean cuisine for us. It was May, so it wasn't that hot, but I told people to bring swim stuff if they wanted to swim. Joe was able to get their cousin Rose to bring their aunt Ruby, who had been living in Atlanta. They hadn't seen her since the wedding.

It had been a month since we got the news of Sean being the father of this other child, and I was still trying to deal with it all. It had been so hard planning this party for him because I was hurt. So, I had been focusing on doing it for Twin since she was going through so much. She had her good days and bad days. Some days, she got very sick with flu-like symptoms, and other days, she'd be out on the move with Jo'el, which I loved for her. I prayed she'd have so many more days like that.

Since she was still refusing to start chemo, she had been doing monthly tests to make sure it wasn't spreading. Last week, she had minor surgery, which kept her down for the weekend, but then she was right back to work. I could never tell if she was getting better or worse—all I could do was love on her while she was here. As her sister-in-law and godmother to her child, I tried to go over there as much as possible and help out when she was having a down day. I didn't know if I was doing it out of the kindness of my heart or selfishly to get away from my husband sometimes. My heart broke whenever I heard about this new child and when he spoke the mother's name. The baby was due next month, and he'd been going to appointments, talking to her daily on the phone. I think he thought it was okay because he did it in front of me and not behind my back, but it wasn't. I got that he wanted to include me. Before he did it, he asked me to see if it was okay, but I was sick of the whole situation. He even asked if we could go to the baby shower, which she had last week on Mother's Day. That type of insane shit he did pissed me off. Again, I didn't think he meant any harm, but he didn't think about how much this shit hurt me. Needless to say, we did not attend the baby shower—absolutely the fuck not. I told him to send a gift to her house because what the fuck was he thinking?

I swear, having sex was my only coping mechanism. It was the only time when he just shut the fuck up about the whole situation. It was the one time where it was just me and him and when we were so connected that nothing in the outside world mattered. The way he took care of all my needs in bed was the same way I wished he would take care of my heart outside of bed. But he just didn't or wouldn't recognize my pain.

"Mom?" Sky came into my room while I was getting dressed.

"Yes?"

"Ryan is here."

"Great. Help him find whatever he needs. Show him where the grill is. The coals and fuel are already out there. Tell him I'll be down in a few. Have you heard from your father or Joe?"

"Yes, Uncle Joe is on his way here, and I talked to Pops. They just got to breakfast, and he told me to tell you they're going to the cemetery to put flowers on their mom's grave after, so that buys us some more time."

"Fantastic. Kelly is on the way, so keep a lookout."

"Got you," she said before leaving.

"Thank you."

When Joe arrived, he and Lil Sean finished setting up the tables and chairs outside as I fed my beautiful goddaughter. Aunt Ruby was the first guest to arrive. She came in with her walker, moving about as slowly as a snail.

"Sean sure has come a long way since that heifer, Makayla," she said slowly, dragging down the hall. All I could do was laugh, but I was glad Lil Sean was outside. I would never let anyone speak ill of his mother in front of him.

Rose shook her head in shame. "I'm so sorry. She has no filter. This 90-year-old lady is off her rocker," she laughed. "Hey, girl," she said, giving me a hug.

"Tiera. Hey baby, your house is beautiful," Aunt Ruby said as I gave her a big hug.

"Thank you, Aunt Ruby. Would you like anything to drink?"

"No, thank you, honey. That's quite all right. I have a bladder weaker than a pair of kitten heels on a fat lady." Rose and I looked at each other and laughed. "Who's little girl is this?" she asked, touching Jo'el's hand.

"This is Twin's daughter, Jo'el."

She looked at me as if she was trying to remember something. "Wow, that's amazing! Finally, she's here. We've waited so long for you, precious. Rose, could you please take me to the couch so I can sit down and cuddle this little one? Good for Twin." Rose walked Aunt Ruby over to the couch. For a 90-year-old woman, she moved around pretty well. She was so cute—all old and wrinkly. She had really thick gray curly hair for her age. I hoped Sean had those genes and would pass them on to our children. My mom was already thinning at the top of her head, so there was no luck on my end.

I sat Jo'el on Aunt Ruby's lap, and she was overjoyed.

"Tiera, where are your two at?" My anxiety went from 0 to 100 when she asked that.

"They must be, like, nine now, right?"

I was so relieved when she said that. I didn't want to go into the miscarriage— not now, not today.

"It's been so long since the wedding," she continued.

"Yes, yes, it has, and they are six now. They'll be seven in July. They're outside running around." I turned to Sky. "Sky, can you tell them to come see Aunt Ruby?" She nodded and went to get them.

"That's your daughter, too, right?"

"Yes, that's Skylar. She's a grown little lady now."

"Yes, she is. So beautiful." She signaled me to come closer. I bent down, and she whispered in my ear. "I'm so sorry for your loss, baby." Then she kissed me on my cheek.

"Thank you, Aunt Ruby. That means a lot."

The twins came running in to meet Aunt Ruby.

"Whoooa," she spoke, taken aback by how big they were. They gave her hugs and kisses.

"Watch the baby's head, guys," I said to the twins. They were both just so rough at times.

Right after, Lil Sean walked in from out back with Sky.

"Oh my! Now, I already know who this is. My God, you're the spitting image of your father. Come on and give Aunt Ruby some sugar." He walked over, hugged her, and kissed her on the cheek. "If only your grandmother could see you now. If your grandmother were here, you all would be spoiled rotten," she told them.

As she went on telling them about their grandmother, I left them talking and showed Rose around.

After the little tour, everyone started to pour in. I took a look at Sean's location, and they were only 10 minutes away. They thought they were having a typical, casual dinner with the family, but they didn't know that we had invited some of their co-workers and Aunt Ruby.

When Sean and Twin walked in, they were very surprised. Twin started crying when she saw Aunt Ruby. She was the closest family member to them after their mom died. She was actually their mother's aunt. When the party started, Sean took my hand and told me to follow him upstairs. I prayed that it wasn't about his baby mom. He was dumb enough to ask if she could attend the party. I swear, I would go off if he did.

Once we got in the room, he showed me a box.

"It was in the mailbox," he said.

"Is it?"

He nodded yes and smiled.

"Our babies." My heart felt so content.

We had gotten the twins cremated together, which took about two months to get to us. When we got their ashes, it was very hard on all of us. The reality of it all had sunk in. That day, I was a wreck. I cried, Sean cried, and even Skylar and Lil Sean cried. Then we found a place that would turn their ashes into two stone hearts—one for me and one for Sean—in Los Angeles.

That took two more months, and now they were finally here. I breathed in and exhaled deeply. He brought me over to the bed; we sat down, and he opened it.

There were two boxes, each containing stone hearts. They were about 5 inches in size, not too big, with "Heaven" and "Halo" engraved at the top, their birthday dates listed under their names, and "Forever in Our Hearts" written on the back. I held mine in one hand and gently caressed over the top with the other, feeling each letter in their name. "My babies," I said softly. With everything that had been going on, I was just happy to have my babies home. Even though they weren't here in physical form, it gave me a little peace. They weren't traveling around in boxes all over the country. They were home. We both teared up, but we didn't cry.

"I love you so much, T. Thank you for still hanging in here with me, bae. Thank you for everything," he expressed with sincerity. I could sense the depth of his feelings, and it was clear that he truly meant what he said. Even though I was still hurting, he meant the world to me.

"I love you too," I responded softly, gazing into his eyes before kissing him.

"Real quick?" he whispered, pointing a few times with his head in the direction of the bed.

I laughed, "Umm, no." I pushed his face back.

"Fine! Okay, okay, not in front of the babies," he said with a smile, holding his stone heart in his hands. He gently put the heart back in the box, took it over to his side of the bed, gave it a kiss, and then placed it on his nightstand, leaving the box open.

"I'll close it tonight when you, you know, give me some birthday loving. They don't need to see or hear that."

I laughed again. "Shut up."

He chuckled. "Something is really wrong with you., I swear," I say, putting mine on my nightstand as he makes his way back over to me. As he approached, I stood up.

He grabbed my hand and pulled me closer to him. "You ready, old man?" I asked.

"Let's do this, little mama."

We headed downstairs to the party. We ate, danced, and some people smoked. The food was terrific. Ryan made oxtails, curry goat, rice and peas, and cabbage before going outside to grill jerk chicken, which everyone lined up for when it was done. Tiff, as a Jamaican, approved of his cooking. Kelly's boyfriend's mixed drinks were incredible. He had a southern peach tea drink made with Crown Royal for Twin. It was called the Island Redemption, which she had enjoyed at least two so far. She said she pumped enough milk for two months to enjoy her day, and I loved that for her. For Sean, it was a simple mule made with Tito's, which was Sean's go-to drink when he didn't have a beer, but it was green in color and called Ja'makin Me High. Sean loved it. He was definitely going to be drunk soon.

While Twin and I were in the kitchen talking, Sean's phone started ringing. Twin and I looked at it but continued talking and enjoying ourselves. We kept smiling and laughing, having such a good time. His phone rang again, and I just grabbed it and looked at it.

It was Megan. She texted him: "I forgot it was your birthday. Happy birthday, Sean." Okay, I can deal with that. It's his birthday. But then she sent him a picture of her belly with "Happy birthday, daddy" written underneath. This was the kind of thing that pisses me off. They were both idiots because *why*? He really needed to check her. I tossed the phone back on the countertop and excused myself from Twin. I had to leave before I started crying in front of everyone. I grabbed my keys and my phone and headed outside to the car. As I was about to back out of the driveway, Twin stopped me and got in the car. She looked at me and put her hand on the steering wheel.

"I don't know where you're going, but I just know you're not okay. I read the text messages. So whether it's just somewhere to get some air and clear your mind, or it's to pull up on that hoochie, I'm riding. You're my sister, and I'm down for whatever. So..." She sat back and put her seatbelt on. "Let's go."

I smiled, said nothing, and backed out of the driveway. I drove to a lake that was about 15 minutes away from the house. I parked, and we just sat there for a while, looking out at the water. I felt like we were both just sitting with our own thoughts. About 10 minutes later, I spoke.

"The twins' hearts came in today," I said, still staring out into the lake.

"That's amazing. I know you're relieved. I'm so happy you got them. It took forever. Are you happy with how they turned out?" Twin asked.

"Yes, very."

"I never made it far enough to give birth or have anything to hold on to. The longest I carried a child was about seven weeks. I never needed any medical attention. It was as though, as soon as I found out I was pregnant, I miscarried," she expressed.

I put my hand on top of hers, and she put her other hand on top of mine. We just sat there quietly for a few moments.

"Twin, what do I do?"

"Heal? That's the only thing you can do. How you heal is up to you. But heal for Tiera and no one else. Heal in the way Tiera needs to heal."

"The cheating... yeah, it hurt me, but this baby..." I laid my head back on the headrest. "This baby kills me. But what kills me the most is that Sean doesn't even acknowledge my pain." I wiped a tear from the corner of my eye before it dropped. "And when it comes to this woman, he acts like a fucking idiot. I understand there's a baby on the way. Okay! But it's not here yet. She's been doing fine for the last six or seven months by herself. All of a sudden, she needs so much help. Mind you, my babies would have been born a week or two after hers. But then he asks me if I want to go to her damn baby shower *on* Mother's Day! Am I being selfish?" I looked to her. "Please let me know if I am."

"Fuck no!" she yelled. "Joe and I were blown away when he said he asked you that shit. I couldn't believe it. Joe even got up and just left the room. Of course, I talked to him. But he's never wrong and knows it all. That's why I say stop living for him and live for yourself. Sean has to grow up—he's fucking 40!" Twin replied.

"I keep thinking to myself, if I was just around more, this would have never happened," I said.

"STOP! I will not sit here and let you blame yourself, Tiera. No! You were out there doing what you had to do for your family. *He* fucked up, not you. He must own up to his shit, all of it. Just because you took him back doesn't give him a pass for it. This is a whole other ball game. A child is coming. I get that he's trying to be Mr. Nice Guy and please everyone, but you should be the only one he needs to please and get things right with before anyone else. Sorry to say, but before the child, too, at this point. You are his wife. I'm not telling you to end your marriage at all, but if your glass is half empty from pouring yourself into this situation, who is pouring back into you? Girl, don't let your cup run dry. He laid down with that woman, let him make it right. To tell you the truth, I don't even think it's his. There's something funny about this story, but hey, what can I say to DNA? Sean has to grow up and step up. I'll take the blame for his lack of growth. I've been his sister and mother. I've been fixing his problems and protecting him. I told him he needed to start figuring things out on his own. I may not be here much longer."

"Don't say that." I looked at her and squeezed her hand.

"Tiera, it's true. I haven't been honest with everyone. But…" Tears started to run down her face. She took her shirt and wiped her eyes. I immediately started crying as well. I've never seen Twin this vulnerable. "…It's spreading quickly. I'm starting chemo next month. I've been pumping milk like crazy for Jo'el. I want her to stay on it at least until she's one, which is only four months from now."

"Where has it spread to?"

"My lungs. That's what the minor surgery was for a few weeks ago—to see how much of my lungs it spread to. Thankfully, there's not much coverage, but I need treatment."

I grabbed her and hugged her. I couldn't begin to imagine her real pain. She's so strong; I would literally fall apart knowing something like that.

"I'm so sorry, Twin. Whatever you need, you know I'm here for you."

"I've come to terms with whatever is meant to be, will be. So don't feel sorry for me. The one thing I wanted out of life, I got.

Whether I'm here with her until she's 80 years old or until she's 13, I wouldn't change my decision. She is happy, healthy, and strong."

"When are you going to tell Sean? He would be so pissed if he found out I knew and didn't tell him."

"I told him today I'm going to start chemo next month. He was so happy, and I told him I wanted him to go to my first appointment with me. So I'm going to tell him then."

"Okay, good."

She wiped her eyes again. "I guess I needed to clear my head, too," she said, laughing.

"Thank you for coming with me and thank you for everything. You are the sister I never thought I needed. Thanks for all the help with the twins and getting them in school. Helping Skylar become an amazing teacher. You have taken her in and have been the best aunt."

"That's my baby, and by the way, she knows. I tell that girl everything. She has really been a piece of my heart I didn't know I was missing."

"That girl can keep a secret, can't she?"

"I'll tell her stuff before I'll tell Joe." We laughed.

"Speaking of the guy, here he goes now." She answered her phone.

"Hey babe... Tiera and I ran out for a second... I wanted to tell her." She looked over to me and smiled. I smiled back at her.

"Yeah, I'm okay. We're about to head back now... Okay... I'll tell her... Love you too, bye."

"Your dumb husband called you."

"I didn't hear anything." I grabbed my phone from the back seat. "Oh, Lord. I grabbed someone else's phone. This isn't even mine. I think it's Rose's."

"I bet. You were heated. I thought we were really going to that lady's house." Twin said

"Really? I'm not even that type of person."

"I didn't think so in the beginning, but after that day you found out Sean cheated on you, and you fucked him, the house, and his car up, and then said fuck the cops when they told you to drop the bat... I knew you weren't to be played with." We chuckled. "When Joe and I got home, he said, 'Oh, Sean got Tiera fucked up. He fucked around and found out.'"

I had to stop backing out of the parking space to finish laughing. "That was embarrassing."

"I think the only person embarrassed was Sean. The whole block knew he was a cheater and that his wife whipped his ass."

We laughed the whole ride back to my house.

Before we got out of the car, I turned to Twin and said, "Remember years ago when you popped up at my house asking me to give your brother a chance?"

"Oh my goodness, yes." She shook her head. "I'm sorry."

We laughed again.

"No, thank you! Stuff happens in marriages all the time, but without you, my family wouldn't have existed. Cheating husband and all. I'm grateful to you. You saw what he and I could become way before we became it. I love you, Twin."

"I love you too, girl." We hugged and then exited the car.

Sean came outside as I closed the driver's side door. "Where y'all been?"

"Out," Twin said, walking past him and into the house.

"Where'd you go?" He came up to me and wrapped his arms around my waist. He's drunk. I can smell it all on him.

"Girl stuff."

I wanted to speak with him about the text, but it's pointless right now. It's his birthday, so I'm going to let him have this one.

"I missed you." He said, kissing my neck.

I stopped him from kissing me and held his face up. "You can show me how much you miss me later. Come on, let's get back to the party," I said.

"Yes, ma'am." He replied.

The rest of the night was fantastic. Ryan made a three-layer cheesecake for them with vanilla bean on the top, cookies and cream in the middle, and red velvet at the bottom. It was spectacular. After the cake, we went outside and gave them their gift, which they were thrilled with.

"That's not even the best part," Joe said.

"Shit, what's the best part? I need to know now!" Sean added.

And we all pulled out our passports.

"IT'S A GROUP TRIP!" Tiff said, sticking her tongue out and waving her passport.

The guys—James, Mally, and Joe—shook up bottles of champagne and popped off the corks, spraying everyone like we were in a locker room celebrating an NBA playoff Championship. The kids loved it, laughing and trying to dodge the champagne bursts, and it ended up being a great time. The energy was infectious, and for a moment, all the day's tension melted away. Everyone enjoyed the celebration, and for a few hours, we were able to forget about everything and just be present in the joy of the moment.

How Have You Been?
Twin

Chapter Playlist

☒ ALICIA KEYS—"Tell You Something"

☒ NORMANI FEAT. CARDI B—"Wild Side"

☒ ALICIA KEYS—"Like You'll Never See Me Again"

☒ PATTIE LABELLE—"You Are My Friend"

☒ KINDRED THE FAMILY SOUL—"Where Would I Be"

☒ ALICIA KEYS—"Troubles"

I wasn't feeling my best today. I had been dealing with a cough that came and went, but I was still excited to be surrounded by my family and friends on our vacation to Jamaica. All my nieces and nephews were there, along with my friends and their partners. I was mostly excited to have this time with Jo'el. She was only eight months old and already leaving the country.

"Our mom was never able to take us out of the country. Heck, we barely made it to Clementon Amusement Park in New Jersey. I was grateful that I had the opportunity to share this time with her. Even though she wouldn't remember it, I knew I'd cherish this for as long as I lived. I hadn't been out of the country since Joe and I went on our honeymoon to Jamaica. I always felt at peace when I was there.

We took our bags to the room when we arrived at the resort, then, the girls, the kids, and I headed straight to the beach because I didn't want to waste any time. The guys went to the pool to sit at the swim-up bar.

"Why have we never done this?" Kelly asked.

"What, boo?" Tiff replied.

"Go on group vacations? It's not like we're the type of friends who can't get everyone together. With over 20 years of history, why haven't we planned anything before?"

"I have no idea, but I'm glad we're doing it now," Tiff said.

Kelly was absolutely right. Throughout all these years, all the birthdays, and all the ups and downs, we'd never had the chance to travel out of the country together. It was truly astonishing how we often believed we had all the time in the world to create memories with our loved ones, only to realize that tomorrow was never guaranteed for anyone. [⏸ **"Tell You Something"** by **ALICIA KEYS**]

"Aunt Twin, can you bury me in the sand like we used to do?" Lil Sean asked.

"Of course I can."

"Can you do us too, Auntie Twin?" TT asked.

"Of course, I can do you too."

Skylar reached out to take Jo'el.

"Thank you, love."

"Alright, who's first?" I asked, walking out into the sand to dig holes for the kids.

I hadn't done this since we used to take Lil Sean to Ocean City, Maryland, when he was little. It was all the little things that hurt me to think I wouldn't be here to enjoy them.

We stayed on the beach until the sun went down, laughing, relaxing, letting the sun soak into our melanin skin, and playing with the kids in the ocean. We would've stayed out there even longer if the men hadn't come complaining to us that they were hungry, as if they were children who couldn't feed themselves. The day was perfect and unforgettable.

The following day, I woke up early to watch the sunrise over the ocean from our balcony. It was stunning.

"Babe, what are you doing up so early?" Joe asked.

"Isn't this beautiful, honey?" I replied.

He stretched and stepped out onto the balcony, still in his underwear. "Oh, you're feeling free, huh?" He came up behind me, wrapped his big, strong arms around me, and kissed me on the cheek.

"It is beautiful, babe, but standing here with you is breathtaking," he said as I hugged him tighter.

"You're so sweet. If something happens to me, will you be this sweet to your next wife?"

"Seana, come on," he said, annoyed and letting go of me.

"What?" I grabbed his arm. "I'm just asking, honey. I think it's something we need to talk about. I want you to date, for Jo'el's sake."

"I'm never going to love or be sweet to another woman because you're going to be here, annoying me forever. Until we're old and gray, and long after I'm gone, you're going to be here with our daughter." He took me back into his arms.

"Well, can I date when you're gone?" I laughed.

"No!"

"But…" He squeezed my lips closed with his hand.

"Shut it up," he said, before kissing and licking on my neck. He dropped his drawers.

"Oh, right here?" I asked, taken aback by how carefree he was.

"Yes!"

"Where do you want me?" I asked, and he turned me around and bent me over the balcony. He lifted up my robe and slid down my panties. My big teddy bear of a husband made me feel so alive, carefree, and loved. I couldn't scream. Sean's room was on one side of us, Skylar and her boyfriend were on the other side, and Tiera's mom was below us. So, I bit down on his forearm to mask my moans. Joe liked the pain anyway; it excited him. [⬚ **"Wild Side" by NORMANI feat. CARDI B**] As soon as we both climaxed, Ms. Jo'el started crying.

We both shared a laugh. "I'll get her," Joe said as he picked up his draws. We stepped back into the room. Joe put on his robe, washed his hands, and then went to pick up his princess. I made her bottle so Joe could feed her while I hopped in the shower.

When I got out of the shower, both of my babies were asleep. Jo'el was tucked inside Joe's robe, lying on his chest. I needed to beat this cancer so I could be here with them and for them. I took a picture and curled up beside them. My bear and my cub. [⬚ **"Like You'll Never See Me Again" by ALICIA KEYS**]

We slept for a good half an hour before the group text messages started going off.

Today 8:30 AM

Mally

> Hello, hello, grand rising. Breakfast started at 8, where y'all at? I just unloaded, now it's time to load up with food.

Kelly Girl

> Nasty, Kenny and I are getting dressed now.

Tiffy Boo

I already ate, lol.

Kelly Girl

Wow.

Mally

That's my girl, Tiff, is ya mouth looking like a glazed donut.

Tiffy Boo

Never, I don't waste, just taste.

Me

Well, my stomach hurts.

Kelly Girl

Aww, I'm sorry, boo. Do you know what it hurts from?

Me

From getting bent over the BALCONYYYYY!

Tiffy Boo

AYYYYYYYYYY, period, boo!!!!

Mally

Aht a girl. That's why the building was shaking, Joe's King Kong ass thrusting.

Tiffy Boo

CTFU, it's too early.

Husband

That was just my dick hitting the floor when I pulled out.

Tiffy Boo

Yoooooooooo, I'm outta here, lol.

Mally

Ayo, you wild for that, Joe. I don't wanna know about your meat before I eat breakfast.

Kelly Girl

Am I the only one who didn't have sex this morning?

Mally

No, Sean ain't getting no pussy with all those kids in the room.

Pickle Head

FUCK YOU.

Tiffy Boo

HAHAHAH, where is James? James, wake yo ass up.

Pickle Head

We gonna go eat or what? The room service was trash last night.

Me

That sucks. I'm going to need a few. Joe just got in the shower and I'm getting the baby ready.

Pickle Head

Let's meet at like 9:45.

Mally

Ard.

Kelly Girl

K.

James

Sorry, I was getting topped off, lol.

Mally

That's my boy, ok Lay. That's how you treat a man in the morning. Kelly and Sean came on vacation to collect seashells?

Tiffy Boo

HAHAHAHAH.

Pickle Head

FUCK YOU.

Kelly Girl

First off, Kenny can't drink and y'all got him fucked up, nor can he hang. His ass was drunk and went to sleep.

Tiffy Boo

You should've sat on his face while he was asleep, he would've woke up.

Mally

Or died, wtf Tiff.

Tiffy Boo

Lol, he would've been fine.

Mally

We going down to get a table for everyone, see y'all down there.

As we walked out of our room, Sean and Tiera came out of theirs. The twins ran over to see Jo'el in her stroller.

"Hey, hey, family."

"Hey, hun," Tiera said.

"Where is Lil Sean?" I asked as we all walked down to breakfast together. Joe and Sean were ahead of us. The twins were pushing the stroller, and Tiera and I were in the back.

"He's with my mom. He didn't want to stay with us. He's getting too old to hang with us, I guess. Plus, Mom got the suite with the swim-up pool. She said they were out there all night just chilling."

"Aww, Gram Gram and her boy. I'm so glad he gets to experience having a grandmother."

"Yeah, I called to see if they were going to breakfast with us, and they had already eaten and were on their way to the waterfall with Skylar and her boyfriend."

"Well, damn."

"My mom doesn't play on vacation; she's going to be out there doing everything she's big enough to do."

"As she should, go head mama A."

When we got outside, everyone was out there waiting on the trolley to take them to breakfast.

"How long y'all been out here waiting?"

"Ten hot-ass minutes," James said.

"Y'all wanna walk?" Sean asked.

"Nigga, I'm on vacation, I'm not tryna walk," James said.

"Why not? Didn't Jesus walk to Nazareth in those same sandals you've got on? Are you better than Jesus now?" Sean said, and we all started laughing. Even the other people waiting at the trolley stop were laughing. James jumped on Sean to put him in a headlock.

"You better be lucky your children are here," James said as Sean was laughing so hard, he started to tear up.

"You can't take these big kids anywhere. Come on, Twin," Kelly said, interlocking her arm with mine as we took off to breakfast, just like we used to do on our way to the dining hall in college.

The walk was about a mile. It wasn't even that long, but I enjoyed the time walking with all my loved ones, playing, joking, and laughing. I preferred that over a ride any day.

Once at breakfast, Mally was able to reserve a private room for us. Thank God, because when we got together, we were a loud bunch.

"Bae, what do you want? I'll go make your plate," Joe asked.

"Nope," I shook my head, "No, you will not, honey. I'll go and make the plates because you always come back with all this extra, unwanted stuff."

"It's a buffet. You're supposed to try everything while you're on vacation."

"Honey, just tell me what you want. I'll go make yours first."

"Fruit, pancakes, eggs, you know, all the regular stuff, and see if they have some curry goat and rice, stuff like that."

"See, that's what I mean—pancakes and goat?!" I looked at him in disbelief because why would he want that? It didn't even sound good. So extra. "I'll see what they have."

"Thanks, honey. I love you," Joe replied.

As we all sat down to eat, I noticed there was tension between Sean and Tiera. Something must have happened during that short time. About halfway through the meal, Sean's phone rang. He denied it, but I could tell by Tiera's body language that she was very annoyed by the call. I had a feeling it was the baby mama, and if I were Tiera, I would've been annoyed too. Then, his phone went off again.

"Answer the phone and set some fucking boundaries," Tiera said quietly and firmly as I eavesdropped.

"What am I supposed to say?" Sean asked.

"What do you mean, what are you supposed to say? Tell her you're on vacation with your wife and family, and if it's not about the baby being born, everything else is irrelevant. Why do I have to give you a damn script?"

His phone rang again, and he answered it. I could tell everyone was eavesdropping as it got a little quiet when he answered.

"Hey, Meg, what's up?" I looked at Tiera as she watched him talk to the phone. "Yeah, I think that's cute. But look, I'm gonna hit you up when I get back in the States. You know how service is... Ok, bye."

I could see in Tiera's face she was pissed. Her legs were just shaking. I could tell she was trying to calm herself down. I could see her breathing and exhaling deeply.

Sean put the phone down. "There, are you happy? She's not going to call back," he said. I just put my head down in shame.

Tiera stopped shaking and stared at him. "Are you still fucking her?" She leaned over the table and asked him quietly, looking confused.

"No! Can you relax? I'm just trying to do right by everyone," Sean said.

Tiera gave a face of disgust and then chuckled. "It's funny how you're trying to do right by every fucking body when *I'm* the only one you did wrong," Tiera yelled. She then got up from the table and walked out.

Even though everyone was eating, we all glanced at each other. It was an awkward silence. I looked over at Sean. "You need to grow up." I got up and handed Joe the baby.

"Where you going?" Joe asked.

"I'm going to see about my sister. Someone needs to care about her feelings," I said as I looked at Sean and rolled my eyes.

"Hold up, Twin," Tiff said, as Kelly, Lay, and Tiff's girlfriend got up and came with me. As we were leaving, I could hear James say to Sean, "You fucking this up for all of us."

When we got outside, we jogged to catch up to Tiera. She moved fast.

"Tiera, wait up," Lay said.

She turned around and stopped.

"You don't have to come with me. I'm okay, really. I'm just going to go back to the room and lie down."

"No, you're not. Fuck that! We're about to go get some drinks and be on vacation like we came to do," Tiff said.

"I don't know about y'all, but I've been feeling a little adventurous. Y'all trying to ride on some ATVs?" Lay asked.

"Yes! I think that's what we need—a little rush," I said. We all agreed that it would be perfect.

"Girl's day! Should we ask Mally's chick?" Kelly added.

"We don't know her. Shit, Mally barely knows her," Tiff said.

"I'm going to text him and ask," I said.

"Okay, well, I have to go get some sneakers if we're riding," Tiera said.

"Yeah, me too," I added.

"Well, y'all go ahead, I'll go to the front desk and get us a cab to take us there," Lay said.

"Bet! And Mally said him and the girl are going on a boat ride, so she's out."

"You okay with leaving Joe with the baby?" Kelly asked.

"Of course! My man has this. He may have her looking a bit crazy when I get back—flower shirt, polka dot pants, and red shoes," I chuckled. "But he's got her," I said.

Once we got to the ATVs, I started feeling a little nervous. I had never driven one of these before. I used to hate it when Sean would ride his ATV, worried about his safety. However, we ran into Mama Anderson, Sky, and Lil Sean, who were waiting on their bikes. Seeing Mama Anderson doing something like this at her age gave me the confidence to do it too. We were able to get bikes together and take a ride as a group. I think it was just what Tiera really needed. She was able to ride alongside her two oldest children and her mother. The rush gave me what I needed as well. I felt fearless. We went through muddy waters, up sand hills, and through a jungle. It was amazing—laughing and yelling with my girls. After the ATVs, we all went out to dinner, then Mama Anderson and the kids said their goodbyes.

"We're going zip-lining tomorrow. If you old ladies want to join," Mama Anderson said as she started walking out of the restaurant.

"Oh, we down, Mama A!" Tiff yelled.

"Tiera, I'm hanging out with your mom for the rest of the trip," I said, and we laughed.

After dinner, the girls and I treated ourselves to a relaxing massage at the spa, followed by some much-needed relaxation in the Himalayan salt pool. Since we were all so relaxed, it felt like the right time to share my secret with them.

"Hey, since we are all here, I would like to share something with you."

"Sure, boo," Kelly said. Everyone stopped what they were doing and came closer to me. I took a deep breath. It was hard for me to go through this, but it was even harder for me to share the information with the people I loved. It hurt me to hurt them, but they needed to know.

"There's no easy way for me to tell you all, so I'm just going to come out and say it. My cancer has spread to my lungs." They all looked at me with worry in their eyes. "Buzz kill, I know, right?" I chuckled a little. "I'm starting chemo next month to stop any further growth, then having surgery to remove any cancer that's left on my lungs."

Kelly started breaking down in tears. "I'm so sorry, Twin. I'm so sorry, boo," Kelly said as she wrapped her arms around me and hugged me. I didn't want to become emotional, so I sucked it up and stayed strong.

"Who all knows?" Tiff asked.

"Just Joe and everyone here. I'll tell the guys after I tell Sean."

Tiff stayed strong, reassuring me that I could overcome this. At that moment, we all came together in the pool, forming a comforting group hug, with Lay and Ebony joining in to show their support. [🎵 **"You Are My Friend" by PATTI LABELLE**]

"The Lord is not going to let you leave us here alone with Sean," Tiera said, and we laughed. Tiera gave me a wink. I was happy that she was able to defuse the emotional situation.

"Oh no, the Lord knows that's just way too much for us to bear. You are the only soldier strong enough for that one-man army," Tiff said.

"Leave my brother alone. He's not that bad. He just doesn't listen."

"No, he is absolutely rotten because you always coddle him," Kelly adamantly remarked. Tiera nodded and agreed.

"I know, I know. I created a problem. But Sean was very sensitive growing up. So, I always protected him."

"Tiera, has he called you?" Lay asked.

"I left my phone with TT."

"Period," Tiff said.

"So, are you two okay? What happened, if you don't mind me asking?" Lay asked Tiera.

"It's frustrating! This 'baby mama' that Sean now has is constantly calling and texting him.

"For months, she was fine being alone, but now she wants him involved in everything—from the baby shower to picking out names. It's making me uncomfortable. Sean needs to establish boundaries with her, and he's not doing it."

"DNA or not, it just doesn't sit right with me," Kelly said.

"You want me to put her in her place?" Tiff added.

"Sean needs to do his job and separate his wife from his baby's mother. She needs to understand her place. It's really getting on my nerves that all he wants to do is play nice. Since we got here, it's been non-stop, and it's infuriating. That's why I asked him if he was still sleeping with her."

"Bitch, the baby's not even here yet. He's with his family, hoe. Don't let her call around me because I'm telling her off," Tiff continued.

"No, Tiera is right. As a man and a husband, he needs to handle it." I added.

"You got to tell him, Twin, that's the only way," Kelly suggested.

"I can't keep holding his hand. I did for 40 years. He's grown. He will find his way," I said.

After the spa, we headed back to the hotel. I loved hanging out with my girls; it was much needed. Those women were a breath of fresh air. But I loved spending time with my little princess and my big, black, beautiful king even more. When I got in, Jo'el was already put down for the night, and my honey had set up the room all romantically.

"Sorry, I took so long, honey. We were all over the place."

"Sorry for what?" He walked over to me and put both of his big-ass hands on my face. "It's your birthday, your time. I want you to have fun." Then he kissed me with his big, plump lips. "Did you enjoy yourself?"

"Yes, hun, you would have been so proud of me driving my own ATV."

"Say word, you? Went on one by yourself?"

"I did, I did. We should do it together tomorrow after we go zip-lining with Tiera's mom." I walked over to Jo'el and gave my chocolate drop a kiss.

"Mama A is not zip-lining," he said in disbelief.

"Hun, yes she is. She was ahead of all of us on the ATVs—her, little Sean, and Sky."

"Yo, that's crazy."

"I know, right? But she's living her life to the fullest." I got lost in my thoughts, thinking about whether I was even going to be able to see that age.

"You okay?" Joe asked.

"Yes, honey, I'm fine. Thank you for making the room all cutesy and demure" I chuckled. "You stay trying to get in my panties," I said jokingly, despite trying to hide the tears in my eyes.

"Seana?" He scooped me up in his arms and lifted my chin, so I was looking directly into his eyes. "What's wrong?"

I just gave in.

Deeply emotional, I gasped, "Baby...I don't want to die," as I collapsed into his arms. I'd never felt this overwhelmed before, even when I learned about the spreading. I had always tried to stay strong, telling myself that I could make it, but tonight, it all just came pouring out.

"Aww, baby. I don't want you to die, either." He held me tight, and I could feel his heartbeat.

"I want to see our baby grow and for our marriage to continue to flourish. Baby, I want to grow old with you," I expressed.

"Me too, baby. Me too." He held me and just let me cry it all out.

"Hey, let's not focus on the future and just live in the moment." He took his two big thumbs and wiped both my eyes. "Come on."

He pulled me into the bathroom, where he had run us a bath with bubbles and rose petals. There was champagne, choco-late-covered strawberries, and lit candles.

"Hun, this is so very thoughtful of you. I love you so much."

"I love you too. Come on, let's get in."

"Wait!" I laughed. "Hun, did you clean out this tub?"

He reached next to the side of the tub and pulled up a bottle of cleaner. "I got you, boo." I busted out laughing.

"Babe, where did you get this from?"

"Sean and I went to a market off the resort. That's where I got all this stuff and more."

I pulled on his beard so I could kiss him. "I couldn't have asked for a better husband. You're so thoughtful."

"Come on, before it gets cold." We both got in, turned on the jets, and just relaxed.

"So, did you try to talk some sense into Sean while y'all were out today?"

"No, I told him to leave that girl alone a long time ago," he said, then kissed my shoulder.

"Joseph Amri Davidson! You knew about her?"

"Fuck."

"No! Ain't no 'fuck.'" I turned around to him. "You knew Sean was cheating?"

"I saw him out with the girl at Larry's one day when I went to get you a steak. He told me it was nothing."

"Joe, when a nigga says it's nothing, it's always something." I leaned back on him. "Babe, why didn't you tell me?"

"He asked me not to tell you. Guy code—I had to be loyal to my brother."

"My God, honey, I could've nipped this in the bud before he ruined his life," I said, stressed out.

"He's not your son; you got to let him go through his own shit."

"I know, I know, but—"

"No, no buts."

"Yes, a but Joe. God forbid if I go today or tomorrow, he's going to need her more than he needs any of you. You all are his friends, but Tiera is his person. I'm going to give him some guidance and let him take it from there. As a married man your-self, you should be giving your brother-in-law some guidance, too. You know marriage isn't easy. How many times have you gone to your mom and my mom when she was here for a better understanding of it all? You end up getting comfortable, then you think your partner should know how you feel and think because you've been together for so long. It just doesn't work like that. Marriage is an extra job that you get better at over time. Or you either quit, or you get fired."

"Okay, you're right. Those first few years, I know your mom hated to see me coming. I'll talk to him since I have an MIM."

"MIM?" I asked.

"*Masters in Marriage.*" He said, squeezing me in his arms as we laughed.

We ended up talking and laughing in the bathtub until we were prunes.

He gave me a reason to keep living tonight. [◻ **"Where Would I Be" by KINDRED THE FAMILY SOUL**]

The next day, I spent it with Joe and Jo'el, exploring the island. We went everywhere we could. It was perfect. We took lots of pictures and created many memories. We all came back with tans.

On our last morning, I got up to watch the sunrise again, one last time. As I leaned over the balcony, Sean was already leaning over his.

"Hey, boo, what are you doing up so early?" I asked.

"Wanted to catch the sunrise before we head out. You?" Sean replied.

"Same, I guess. It's a twin thing," I chuckled.

"We're just connected."

"Facts... hey, you wanna go down to the beach?" I asked.

"Uh, duh. Let's get it. I'm going just like this."

"Okay, I'm gonna leave Joe a note, and I'll meet you at the elevator."

"Bet."

Once we got outside, Sean said, "The first one to the water wins." I told him I wasn't a child, and I wasn't running in the sand—but then I took off. Yes, I cheated, but I won.

"Cheating ass," he said.

"Winner, winner, chicken dinner. Don't envy me," I said, skipping through the sand.

Sean ran up to me, picked me up, and put me on his shoulder.

"Say you're a cheater, or I'm throwing you in the ocean."

"Okay, okay... you're a cheater, literally," I said, and he ran into the water with me, then dropped me. The water was so cold, but I couldn't stop laughing. I ran back to the sand.

"That's fucked up, you know that?" he said, walking back to the sand, smiling and wiping water off his face.

"Why? Because I said *literally*?"

"Yes," he said, pushing me to the side.

"You mad or nah?" I chuckled.

"Nah... I fucked up," he shrugged. "There's nothing to say."

"So, who do you love more—Tiera or Megan?"

"What? Why is that even a question? You know I love my wife with all of me, man."

"Then you need to move that way. You're allowing all this unnecessary bullshit to occur with Megan. The baby hasn't even been born yet. Megan needs to understand her role. Apart from you taking care of the baby when it arrives, there is nothing else for you two to talk about. Remember, she chose not to tell you for seven months. So why she wanna be up your ass suddenly throws me for a loop. Please tell me you're not still messing around with her."

"Hell no. But I'm gonna talk to her when I get back."

"Good... Well, while we're out here, there is something I need to tell you."

"You're leaving Joe?"

"What? No, nigga," I laughed. "Why would you ask that?"

"Exactly, why would you ask me if I love Megan over my wife?"

"Boy, I'm trying to be serious right now. You always wanna play. That's what's wrong with you, you know? No, for real now."

I looked out over the ocean into the sunset. "As you know, I'm starting chemo soon."

He clapped and cheered.

I turned to him, looking at him. "Well, the reason why I'm doing chemo is because the cancer has spread to my lungs, and if I don't start now, it's going to get worse."

I looked away, not ready for his reaction. We were all we had. It hurt me to have to tell him something that's threatening my life.

"Yeah, I know."

"What?" I hit him. "Who told you?"

"No one. I looked through your papers after you came from surgery," he said.

He winced as I hit him again. "You can't just invade my privacy."

"Why not? You do it to me all the time," he said.

"Yeah, okay, you're right," I sighed.

As he put his arm around my neck, we faced the water. Memories of our confusion during Mom's battle resurfaced. We were young and lost back then.

"I'm scared, Sean."

"I have never let anything happen to you before, and I'm damn sure not going to start now. We are going to fight this. We are going to beat this. I'm committed to utilizing every possible resource to ensure your well-being." I leaned my head on him. "I've already started researching foods you can try."

"You really are the best brother."

"I know."

"Shut up. Come on, let's go, I'm cold. I'll race you."

He sucked his teeth. "Fuck no..." Then he took off running.

"Cheater!" I yelled.

How Have You Been?, Part 2

Tiera

Exactly one month after our vacation, *she* called just before he was about to leave work.

She was in labor.

He asked me if I wanted to go with him, but I just couldn't. I took the kids to school and spent most of the day crying. I waited for hours for him to call, but he didn't. He didn't even check in with me. Even Twin took the time to check in on how I was feeling, and it prompted him to call me shortly after. I felt like he only called because Twin gave him an earful for not checking up on me. When he phoned, he used FaceTime, which just showed how absent-minded he was. I let it ring until he called me the regular way.

> **Sean**: "Hey."
>
> **Me**: "Hey? That's all you have to say? You've been gone since 5:30 this morning. It's 2 p.m. Why haven't you called me?"
>
> **Sean**: "Bae, I'm sorry. She was in labor, and it took a

while. Then I did the chest-to-chest thing. Time just got away from me."

That's what he said, but what I heard was: T, *relax. I'm having a child with another woman right now. We're spending quality family time together. I'm with my second family, and I'll be home when I can. Why are you bothering us?*

I just hung up and cried some more. That was supposed to be *us* with our babies. How could he not understand or sympathize with the way I was feeling? With his simple-minded ass, I didn't know if I could do this. [◻ **"Troubles"** – **ALICIA KEYS**]

MORE BETTER DAYS

Sean

Chapter Playlist

▶ ALICIA KEYS—"Doesn't Mean Anything"

I felt like I had been working overtime on top of overtime. I now had a five-month-old, so I needed extra money to help Meg out. Yes, I had a beautiful baby girl. Born June 15th, her name was Shiloh, but I called her Fatts because she was so round and looked like a jelly roll. She was amazing and looked just like her mother—her twin. Sometimes, I felt guilty for loving her so much because she was the product of me cheating in my marriage.

I was trying to be a proactive dad. Trying to be a good father and husband had been the hardest thing to do in those past months. I was at Meg's house almost every other day when Fatts was firstborn, and T wasn't feeling it. It caused a few arguments.

So, when Fatts turned four months old, Meg and I agreed that I would take her on the weekends. Meg received alimony from her divorce and found a part-time job working from home, so she was able to stay home with her during the week. It worked out better for all of us.

The other kids loved having her around. They played with her all day long. T dealt with everything very well. As long as we were doing this as a team, she was fine. I thought she was warming up to having a baby around again. She fed her, played with her, and even watched her if I needed to do a few hours of overtime. She was a real team player and the best mom ever.

I even took Fatts over to meet Jo'el a few times. Sometimes, when they were in the playpen together, they made all these noises as if they were two gossiping old ladies. I could already tell they were going to be best friends.

Jo'el had turned one just two months prior, and Twin threw the biggest birthday party ever. It was like something off MTV's *My Super Sweet 16*. Everyone we knew was there—even Aunt Ruby came back for the party. Twin did it really big for her baby.

Twin had been doing very well on chemo and unlike our mom, she was still active and on the go. I told Joe that he needed to make her ass go back to work. Both Twin and Jo'el were always out and about every day—shopping, going to the park, eating out, and doing various activities. She hadn't even lost much hair. If you knew her, you could tell it was thinning a little, but nothing noticeable for five months on chemo.

Two days ago, she finally had her major surgery on her lungs. I hadn't been to see her since she got the surgery, and she was so out of it that she didn't even know I was there. So today, I went up there to see her real quick on my lunch break. Joe said they took half of her right lung to remove the cancer, but surprisingly, she was doing fine. That was my sister soldier.

When I got to the hospital, she was up sitting in the chair eating Jello.

"What are you doing?" I asked as soon as I walked in, smiling because I was just happy she was alright.

"They want me to sit up, so they put me here. They want to discharge me in the morning."

"I know, Joe told me. Shit, they don't give you no time to recover." I walked over, kissed her head, then sat on the bed.

"Don't sit on my bed with your outside clothes, nigga!" she yelled at me, making me jump up. I thought I had sat on a tube or something.

"My bad. Damn. You scared me. Remember, Mom used to hit me with her cane every time I sat down on her bed when she was in the hospital?"

"Sure do! And you still haven't learned yet," she said.

"Cuz it's not a normal house bed, so I forget," I said as I walked over to her windowsill.

"Who got you flowers? Let me find out!" I waved my finger at her. "I'm telling Joe."

"Ummm, my wonderful sister-in-law—your wife!" she expressed.

"Well, isn't that just nice of her?" I said, walking back over to her and pinching her cheek.

"Move, weirdo," she said, slapping my hand away. "How are y'all, by the way?"

"We good. She's on her way to pick up the kids from school; they got out early today."

Out of nowhere, Twin bluntly stated, "Sean, your wife is extremely unhappy, and she's on the brink of leaving you."

"What the fuck, Twin?" I said, looking at her, confused. "You're still in recovery. I come to see how you're doing, and this is what you want to talk about? Why would you say something like that? What do you mean?" I stood in front of her. "No, she's not. She's fine. She hasn't said anything to me. Has she said anything to you?"

"No, but I could see it in her face. It is all a front to keep you happy, but deep down, she isn't happy. I don't know the reason." She paused for a moment. "Let me take that back; I know the reason. It's your cheating ass having a child with someone else."

"What do you mean? She loves Fatts, and she took me back after I cheated. Plus, we are having more sex than we'd had in the past three years. Fatts is like the replacement baby we lost."

She stopped eating her Jello, placed the cup on the table, pushed the table away, sat back in the chair, and shook her head.

"I see common sense just isn't common anymore. We can't be related. Boy, please don't ever say that to anyone else. I just want to slap you myself. Listen to me, please—if you want to keep your wife, figure out how you can fix her pain. It won't be easy because you can't undo what you've done, but seeing her feelings and acknowledging her pain may take you a long way. She's not fine, Sean. How would you feel after losing two children and then having to help raise a child from your husband's infidelity? A child that would've been the same age as your own? Losing a child isn't easy—it's hard as hell. Men don't feel all the pain that women feel. And when she reaches her breaking point, you won't have a wife, Dum Dum. You're having so much sex because that's the only thing reassuring her that she still has you because clearly, you're not doing a good job of it.."

"Thanks for the advice, honey, but I know my wife," I said, laughing. "We're good over here, baby. Don't worry about that. Worry about getting all the way better so you can race me in the sand again. I don't wanna hear nothing about 'Oh, I oNlY gOt A hAlF a LuNg, I cAn'T rUn,'" I mocked her.

She looked at me with her eyes wide and her mouth open. "Fuck you, asshole." She grabbed the empty bedpan off the table and threw it at me. It missed me, and we both laughed. She started coughing and held her chest like she was in pain.

"All right, calm down. See, you always doing too much." I ran over and rubbed her back. "I'm leaving so you can get some rest."

"Lies, nigga. You're not leaving so I can get rest; you're walking out on the conversation."

"And you know this!" I laughed and kissed her on her head. "I'll be back in the morning with Joe to help bring your old ass home."

"Sean... fight for her. That's all I'm going to say," she said right before I walked out.

"Yeah, I got you."

"I love you, picklehead," she said.

"Yeah, yeah," I said waving her off, walking out of the room.

I got in the truck and made a few stops before finally getting off work two hours later, only to realize I had left my phone at the hospital on the bed. I could already hear T's mouth.

When I pulled up, I noticed Mally's car in the driveway. He hadn't told me he was coming through. But then again, I didn't have my phone. I decided to run in really quick, let T know I didn't have my phone, and get Mally to ride back to the hospital with me.

When I walked in the house, T called my name.

"Sean?"

"Yeah, babe," I said, taking off my shoes. "Hey, I left my phone at the hospital," I added as I walked around the corner to the kitchen. T, Mally, and Sky were sitting at the kitchen table.

"Mally Mal, what brings you to these parts, my brother?" I said, opening the fridge and grabbing a beer. I closed the door, and T was standing right behind it.

"Hey, babe," I said.

"Sean..." She took my beer and put it on the counter, then grabbed both my hands. Mally and Sky stood up.

"Yes? What's wrong?" I asked, confused. She began to cry, and as I looked around the room, it became clear that *everyone* had been crying. So, I asked again, "What's wrong?"

"Babe..." She took a deep breath. "Twin passed away."

"No," I said, shaking my head.

"Yes, my love."

"What do you mean? I *just* left her. She was fine—sitting up and everything."

"Joe called. He tried to call you, but your phone was there."

"What... what happened? I just left her, and she was *fine*. What happened?"

Mally came up behind me and put his hand on my back. I shoved him away and let go of T's hands.

"Don't touch me, just tell me what happened. What the hell happened? Where is she?" I demanded, my voice growing stronger.

"She went into cardiac arrest shortly after Joe got there. Joe said she had a blood clot in her lung," T said.

"Take me to my sister."

"Sean, I don't think..." Mally began to say before I cut him off.

"I didn't ask for your opinion. I asked you to take me to my sister," I stated firmly before striding out of the house toward the car. T and Mally followed and got in the car. Mally took the driver's seat, and T got in the passenger seat. Knowing I wasn't fit to drive, I positioned myself in the back, prepared to take over if necessary.

"Mally, if you can't whip this shit..."

"I got you," he said and took off.

I sat back, my heart pounding. I couldn't cry because, to me, nothing had been confirmed yet. I was just with her two hours ago. *It couldn't be.* The whole ride was quiet, except for when I heard T whisper to Mally that Tiff had just gotten to Joe. The hairs on my arm stood straight up. *I was her twin—I felt what she felt. How come I didn't feel this? She was just a deep sleeper. Yeah, I'd wake her up. She was my sister.* All these things ran through my mind as I sat in silence.

Mally did what he said he would do—he pushed it to the max. We got there in 15 minutes, tops. He pulled up, and I jumped out, with Tiera following close behind. I headed straight to her room without checking in. As I got closer, my stomach dropped repeatedly, like going over hills in a car. I turned the corner and saw Joe sitting in a chair in front of her room, leaning over and holding his mom while crying. While she was recovering, his mom had been there to look after Twin and the baby. A tear fell down my face, but I was still in disbelief. *No, it couldn't be.*

As I walked down the hall, I felt weak and faint. I walked past everyone and went straight into the room. For whatever reason, I was bouncing slightly, like I was nodding to a beat. I walked up to her side, tears flowing.

"She's just sleeping," I said softly as I gently touched her face, giving into my delusion. "She's cold. Let's get her some more blankets. She's sleeping, and she's cold, that's all. She needs to recover," I repeated as I grabbed every blanket I could find and carefully placed them on her.

"Sean, babe, please stop. Come on," Tiera said with concern in her voice.

"She's asleep, T. Look, this AC is on full blast, making her cold. Yo, someone ask them to get some heat in here." I yelled out to the hallway. "She needs some heat," I kept repeating as I tucked her in with more and more blankets. Tiff and Mally came in and tried to pull me out of the room, but I managed to break away from them. I was crying, but it didn't feel real—I was still stuck in a delusion.

"She's fucking cold, and all y'all are just standing around!" I shouted.

Then I grabbed her, and everything clicked when I held her. Her arms fell to the side, and she didn't hold me back.

Tears streamed down my face as I pleaded, "No, no, no, you can't go... I *need* you... I need you. You're my sister... No, God, no. Please, please." I gently rocked her back and forth, overwhelmed by grief. Mally tried to pull me out of the room, but Tiera stopped him, telling him to give me space. I stayed seated, cradling her lifeless body for what felt like an eternity, lost in sorrow and disbelief.

I eventually laid her back on the bed, stood up, and felt a deep emptiness, as if half of me had left my body.

I passed out. When I came to, I found myself in a hospital bed. I hit my head on the arm of the chair where Twin had been sitting earlier, giving me a concussion. Lying in bed, I wished I had gone into a coma. I can't live life without her.

My sister, my twin, my heart, was gone. [▶ **"Doesn't Mean Anything" by ALICIA KEYS**]

Without

Sean

Chapter Playlist
▢ DMX—"Slippin'"
▢ H.E.R—"Sometimes"
▢ FLOETRY—"Sometimes You Make Me Smile"
▢ DONNY HATHAWAY—"Someday We'll All Be Free"

[▢ **"Slippin'" by DMX**] After my sister's passing, I wasn't the same. For a long time, I couldn't eat or sleep. I went on FMLA for three months because I was so depressed. I didn't shave, and I barely washed up. T started sleeping on the sofa; it got *that* bad. I began taking sleeping pills just so I could escape. When T stopped buying them for me, I started ordering them online. I didn't want to be awake. I kept hoping that it would all be a dream when I woke up. I didn't leave the room. I didn't turn on the TV or let the sunshine in. It felt like every day got worse. People tried to come over and talk to me, but I was gone.

T put Lil Sean in therapy because he was grieving, too. He really took it hard, just like me. I was so wrapped up in my own pain that I couldn't help him process his. But every friend I had stepped up in my absence. Tiff helped by watching the kids for T, cooking, cleaning, and even picking up Fatts a few weekends. Mally and James would come by to take out the trash and take Lil Sean to his games. They were like stand-in fathers to my kids. Kelly even came to take Lil Sean back to New York for a weekend to get his mind off things. It helped him get back into the rhythm of life. But for me, it took much longer.

About three months after Twin's death, I started trying to pick myself up. But it wasn't until Joe, who was huge, came over one day and literally pushed my malnourished ass out of bed onto the floor that I started to snap out of it. Once I was on the floor, he opened the curtains and stood in front of me.

"You stink," he said, looking down at me as I struggled to open my eyes. The sunlight was too much for me to handle.

"I know losing Twin was like losing part of you. Trust me, I know. She was my better half, the mother of my child, and now I'm left to raise our daughter alone. I'm just hoping I can do half the job she was doing when she was here. I know it hurts. It hurts like hell. But at some point, you *have* to get up and start living again. After the funeral, I had one week to grieve with my mom and sister here, but after that, I had to start living again for my baby girl. She needed me, just as your family needs you. You can't let them see that you just gave up. You must be strong, even when you don't know how to be. Time waits for no one. While you're stuck in this funky ass room, your life is passing you by. And I know your sister wouldn't want this from you. As a matter of fact, if she could come down here, she'd tell you off. Hell, she's probably the reason I'm here right now. Even in death, that girl must control everything."

I chuckled.

"Yeah, she sent you," I said, sitting up.

"You're my brother, my child's only uncle. I need you to get up. It will always hurt to some degree, but it will get better in time. I still cry every day, but I handle my business because I know that's what she would want me to do. So come on, bro, get up."

He reached out his hand and helped me off the floor, and I felt the weight of everything crash down on me. Tears started falling, both from the pain and the shame of what I had become. Joe pulled me into a hug.

"Damn, my boy, you smell thick—like a pile of trash. I know T isn't giving you any ass smelling like that."

We both laughed. It was the first time I laughed in a long time.

"Now wash your ass and come downstairs. People are coming over. T's making me a goodbye dinner."

"Goodbye?" I asked, confused.

He pulled a key out of his pocket and handed it to me.

"Yeah, Jo'el and I are moving to Maryland to be closer to my family."

"Wait, what? Why? Jo'el is the only person I have that's a part of my sister. You can't take her away from me."

"*I'm* her father, and the decision has already been made. Plus, I can't live in that house without Twin. Hell, I only moved to Philly for her after college. Everything here reminds me of her. I can't stay in her childhood home without her. And if I'm ever really going to move on, I have to do what's best for me and my daughter. We're going to stay with my mom until we find something of our own. There, I'll have the help I need. And I'll have a day or two here and there to continue to grieve my wife when I need to."

"I understand," I said quietly.

"Don't worry. We'll visit and call. Hell, you can take summers if you want. Daddy needs a break," he laughed. "You'll always be her uncle, and we'll always be family. And the house is rightfully yours."

I looked at the key, disbelief still washing over me. "I can't believe you're leaving. This shit is just all fucked."

"It's only fucked if you keep letting your life pass you by," he said. "Now get your ass in the shower and come be with your niece. I'm sure holding her will give both of you what you need.

You two are half of the person we miss the most. Two halves make a whole. You two need each other."

After my talk with Joe, I took a shower, went downstairs, and held my niece. And he was right. When I picked her up, she just stared at me. It felt like we both saw Twin in each other. She wrapped her arms around my neck, and I held her tight. It felt like Twin was in the room with us for that moment. I started to feel like maybe, just maybe, Twin had planned this somehow, from up there, still managing to control the room. [🞂 **"Sometimes" by H.E.R**]

The next day, I was back with my children and wife, laughing and loving them. Tomorrow isn't promised, and I wanted to enjoy every day with them. I even put a crib in the twin's room for Fatts when she came over. I wanted her to be more included in the family. Even though she wasn't conceived with my wife, I loved her like I loved all the rest.

Before I knew it, Twin's birthday and mine were coming up. This would be the first birthday without her. We always did our own thing in the morning—had breakfast and exchanged gifts. It was our tradition after Mom passed. So, I got up early to get breakfast and went to her gravesite. Even though she couldn't give me a gift this year, I brought her flowers. [🞂 **"Sometimes You Make Me Smile" by FLOETRY**]

"Hey, pickle head. I always thought I would go before you or that we'd go together. Damn it, this is hard." I started crying.

"You were supposed to turn up with me this year. If you didn't want to give me a present, that's all you had to say. You didn't have to go on and die. You're always so dramatic." I laughed, even though it didn't feel right. "Shit's not the same without you. Who do I have if I don't have you? All I ever had was you and Mom, and now you're both gone."

As I looked over, I saw T and the kids walking up, followed by James, Lay, Mal, Tiff, Kelly, Joe, and Jo'el. Even T brought Fatts. They all came bearing blankets, breakfast, flowers for Twin, and a gift for me. My heart swelled.

"We all knew how hard today was going to be for you. It's hard for everyone. We just couldn't let you spend it alone," T said.

"Yeah, T called me, and with no hesitation, I was coming," Kelly added.

"Thank you all. You don't know how much this means to me," I said, tears falling again. I kissed T, and everyone joined in for a group hug. What I thought would be one of the worst days of my life ended up not being so bad. We spent the next few hours talking and bringing up old memories. We even had conversations as if Twin were right there with us. [☒ **"Someday We'll All Be Free" by DONNY HATHAWAY**]

Ashes

Sean

Chapter Playlist

▶ DENIECE WILLIAMS—"Free"

▶ TREY SONGZ—"Break From Love"

▶ KIANA LEDE & BRYSON TILLER—"Gone"

▶ THE O'JAYS—"I Can Hardly Wait Til Christmas"

▶ SZA—"I Hate You"

▶ INDIA. ARIE—"Beautiful"

▶ AMERIE—"All I Have"

▶ DVSN—"Thinking About Me"

▶ USHER—"Good Good"

It seemed like this year moved faster than any other year. Fatts had just turned one, and Lil Sean turned 13 in June. The twins turned seven in July, and Jo'el would be two in October. We were also coming up on the one-year anniversary of Twin's passing this November. It was already September. Where had the year gone?

One day, when I got back from dropping off Fatts, T was sitting in the living room with the fireplace on, drinking wine, and vibing to Deniece Williams' song, "Free," which was playing low on the record player. I grabbed a glass from the kitchen, sat next to her and poured myself a glass. I was ready to relax after having Fatts all weekend; that little girl was a handful. T had our wedding photo album on her lap; she must have been reminiscing as she drank her wine and stared into the fireplace. That was a fantastic day.

"I love this song," I said, taking a sip and staring into the fireplace.

From my peripheral vision, I saw that she moved the photo album from her lap.

"I want a divorce," she said.

I turned to her, dismayed, and she handed me an envelope that had been under the photo album.

"A what?" I asked as I opened the envelope. Inside was divorce papers.

"Are you... are you serious?"

"I'm sorry, Sean, this isn't working for me."

I turned to her completely. "Where is all this coming from? I don't understand. I thought we were fine."

"I've been going back and forth about this for about a year now, and it keeps getting harder for me. I'm not happy anymore."

"A year? So that's it? You want to tear our family apart?"

"Please, Sean. *You* did that a long time ago, but I'm not here to argue about the past. What's done is done. I figured you could go stay at Twin's house now that Joe has turned it over to you. We can trade off week to week with the children."

I chuckled. "You want me to go stay somewhere that's going to remind me every day that my sister is gone? You've got to be kidding me."

"I know it is still hard. She died almost a year ago now... Listen, I don't know, Sean. That's for you to figure out. Take the money we were going to use for vacation and get an apartment. But until then, I think it's better if you sleep downstairs."

She got up to walk away.

"Tiera!"

I was so confused. She was telling me she was divorcing me without any explanation, but when she turned to me, it was only then that I finally understood what my sister told me. T was miserable, and I never noticed it until now. I felt her pain in my heart. As much as I wanted to run to her and beg for us to fix whatever was broken, I couldn't. I always wanted what was best for her and my children, and if this was going to give her back that happiness, fine. I disagreed with it, but I would give her time.

"Okay," I said, but I was broken on the inside, and she walked away.

The next day, after work and when the kids got home from school, we sat down and told them I was moving to Aunt Twin's old house. Lil Sean decided he wanted to stay here as his primary home and do every other week with the twins. It broke my heart. I had never been without my son, but I didn't want to make him leave his home just because of me. This whole thing was tearing me up inside.

Two weeks later, I moved out. Of course, my guys, James and Mally came and helped me. The girls—Tiff, her girlfriend, Ebony, and Kelly—went to Twin's house to clean it up. No one had been in it since Joe and the baby left, which had been about seven months ago. I couldn't believe I was losing my home and my family. I couldn't believe this was the end. T took the kids out so it wouldn't be so hard for me to leave with them there. After everything was in the truck, I took one last look at the house and left. [▶ **"Break From Love" by TREY SONGZ**]

After everything was moved in, I sat on the sofa while everyone ate, as I had no appetite.

"Hey," Kelly came by and sat next to me. "You, okay?"

"Fuck no, I lost everything, Kels—my kids, my wife, my sister, my home, my niece. What the fuck am I even here for?"

"AHT AHT..." Tiff walked up, saying, "We're not gonna talk like that. You're here for all of us. You're a blessing in all of our lives. You're here for your children because they adore you. You're here because you made Mally the damn godfather of your kids, and the good Lord is not leaving your children in his hands." I couldn't help but smirk. "And you haven't lost everything. You still have us. Your brothers and sisters will always be here for you. Besides, nigga, *you* cheated on *her*! Then had her taking care of the baby you and your sneaky link had! T will be back—just give her some time."

"Yeah, bro, that's wild. She must really love you if she went for that," James chimed in.

"Exactly. So, give her time to deal with her feelings. She's better than me, though; I would've cut you from your nuts to your butt, nigga would have been sliced wide open."

"Ouch, damn Tiff," I replied, and we all laughed.

"Just think about it like this, bro; I'm sure Megan will come over and see about her vulnerable baby's father," Mally said with a wink.

"Don't listen to him. You're never getting Tiera back if you knock Megan up again. Take this time for you. You need it." Kelly added. [▶ **"Gone" by KIANA LEDE & BRYSON TILLER**]

After that, it was what T had wanted. Week by week, we took turns taking the children, and that was all. We rarely spoke; when we did, it was only about the children. I didn't think too much about it. I focused on getting the house together when I didn't have the kids. I still had $50,000 in the bank that I'd been saving. I took $15,000 of that and fixed up the rooms for the kids when they came over, making the place more of me and less of my mom and Twin. This house had seen a lot. At first, I didn't want to be here. I didn't know how I was going to feel. But surprisingly, it felt like it always had—like home. I felt safe, and it put my heart at ease. I even got really good sleep. I guess this was where I needed to be.

As for the holidays, T invited me over for Thanksgiving, which I was grateful for. It felt good to be able to spend time as a family again. We had never spent the holidays apart, so she decided to have this last one together. However, Christmas was going to be different. She would have the kids in the morning. They would open their gifts there, and then they would come over that afternoon to stay with me for Christmas night. [▶ " I Can Hardly Wait Til Christmas" by THE O'JAYS]

It was the week before Christmas, and tonight was my night with the kids, so I decided to make it extra special for them. They had been asking me if I could get a Christmas tree because they wanted to decorate it. T usually did all the decorating, so they never really got a chance to add their own touch. So, I got four 4-ft trees and one big tree so we could all decorate them however we wanted. I bought tons of bulbs, lights, and ornaments in all colors so they could go crazy. I also brought up Twin and our mother's decorations from the basement to decorate the big tree.

It was around 8 o'clock when T came over with the kids. When they walked in, they saw the trees and got excited. I loved seeing my babies happy.

"Daddy, you got the tree!" TT said.

"Of course I did. And guess what?" I said, picking her up.

"What?" she said, smiling from ear to ear.

"I got everyone their own tree, so you can decorate it however you want. And if you all go upstairs, put your bags away in your rooms, and put on your PJs like daddy's, we can get this party started!"

They all cheered and ran upstairs.

"So, I don't get matching PJs?" T asked.

"It's just for the Johnsons, sweetheart. You want out." I said as I walked to the kitchen and took the cookies out of the oven.

"Touche, sir. Where's Fatts?" she asked.

"Oh, Fatts is sick. Meg didn't want her around everyone," I added.

"I get it. Taj catches anything and everything."

"Facts."

TT and the boys came running down the steps. They were all so excited, even Lil Sean, who's too cool for most things nowadays. TT held up her hands, so I picked her up and put her on my shoulders. She was so excited that she hugged my head tight when she saw the cookies. After that, they all started asking a million questions.

"Daddy, can I have a cookie!" TT yelled.

"Dad, what kind of pizza do we have?" Lil Sean asked.

"Daddy, what movies are we watching?" Taj asked as he turned on the TV.

"Guys, give your dad a minute. Come here and let me take a picture of you. You all look so cute in your matching PJs. We haven't done matching PJs since the twins were born, their first Christmas," T chimed in.

"Yup, when they were little worms wiggling around," I said, wiggling my body.

"We weren't worms, Daddy," TT said, laughing.

"Yes, small, cute little worms."

I waited until T got all the pictures she wanted, and then I started answering their questions. "Yes, to cookies, but after dinner. Pizza options are, of course, cheese for my wonderful twins, pepperoni and mushrooms for my young man, and Taj, my boy, we are watching all the classic Christmas movies tonight—the ones Dad and Auntie Twin grew up on, none of that new stuff."

"Oh, okay," Taj said.

"Okay, guys, come give me a hug. I'm leaving now. Looks like you all are going to have a great night," T said.

"Stay with us, Mommy," TT said.

"Yeah, Mom," Lil Sean added.

"No, tonight is for you and your dad."

"Stay. Come on, have a cookie or two!" I yelled from the kitchen, in the back of my mind, hoping she would.

"Please, please, Mommy. Yeah, please, Mom," they all went over to her and begged.

"Fine, but not too long, and I want both of my cookies now," she added.

My insides were overjoyed. "Coming right up."

Well, let's just say two cookies turned into four cookies, pizza, soda, popcorn, hot cocoa, and candy. "Not too long" turned into shoes coming off, her helping me decorate the big tree, watching movies, and laughing like we never laughed before. We had a marshmallow fight with the kids—marshmallows were everywhere. She stayed so long that the kids fell asleep. After that, we started watching our favorite Christmas movie, *Home Alone*, until she fell asleep.

When the movie was over, which was around 1 in the morning, I started carrying the kids to their rooms, one by one. They were junk food wasted. There was no point in waking them up. It wasn't until I picked Lil Sean up that T woke up because he was lying on her lap. I had to sit him up first before I could grab him. He was not my little boy anymore—his legs were almost as long as mine, and he was heavy. But he was still my baby.

"What time is it?" T asked as I put Lil Sean over my shoulder.

"Like, one something."

"Yikes." She looked at her phone as I started walking over to the stairs.

"You put the twins to bed already?"

"Yes," I replied as I started walking up the steps.

"Would you mind if I came up and gave them a kiss before I left?"

"Sure," I added.

Once at the top of the steps, I pointed to the middle room and said, "TT's in there." She hadn't been up here since I moved in and redid the rooms for the kids. She went into TT's room, then came into the boys' room as I tucked Lil Sean in.

"So, TT and Fatts share a room, and the boys share a room?" she asked as she came in and kissed the boys.

"Yup."

She walked over to me, smiled, and touched my face. "You are the best dad, Sean Johnson. All that you do for your children is amazing." She looked into my eyes, then turned to walk down the hallway.

I grabbed her arm, pulled her back, and kissed her in the doorway. She passionately kissed me, even reaching up to touch my face again with both hands. As I reached to wrap my arms around her, her emotions drastically changed. It was like she snapped back into reality.

"Stop." She pushed back from me and shook her head. "I can't do this with you." She looked into my eyes. "I'm dating someone, Sean!"

Ashes, Part 2

Tiera

I got home at almost two in the morning. I took off my clothes and checked my phone. I had three missed calls from Jerry. How foolish was I to hope that at least one was from Sean? I mean, I had just broken his heart again. I had just told my soon-to-be ex-husband I was dating again. My soon-to-be ex-husband, whom I had the most amazing time with tonight. My soon-to-be ex-husband who adores our children and will do anything and everything to keep them happy. My soon-to-be ex-husband, whom I couldn't even think of a reason for him to be my ex-husband tonight since his bastard love child wasn't there. I didn't look into a little face and see his unfaithfulness. The same hurt in his eyes when I told him I was dating someone was the same hurt I got when I looked at his child. But his kiss... *my God*, his kiss. [▶ **"I Hate You" by SZA**]

The next morning, I heard Sky call my name as she ran up the steps.

"MOM... MOM..." It got louder and louder until she busted through my door.

"Mom, did you know Jerry was outside?"

"Shit!" I jumped up. "What time is it?" I asked, searching for my phone.

"8:30. Did you want me to let him in? I told him I didn't know if you were here."

"Yes, please. He's supposed to be cooking us breakfast. Let him in, show him to the kitchen, and tell him I'll be down in a second."

"Okay," Sky agreed and headed back downstairs.

I jumped up, brushed my teeth, and quickly showered. It was the quickest shower I had ever taken. Just enough to smell fresh. I dried off and returned to the room to find Sky sitting on my bed.

"What's this?" she asked, holding my wedding picture I had taken out of my nightstand.

"What does it look like, nosey?" I said, snatching the picture and putting it back in the drawer.

"What happened at Pops' house?"

"Sky, I don't have time for this. I have to get ready. There's a man in my kitchen doing Lord knows what." I hurried up and put on some sweat shorts, a sweatshirt, and some socks. I threw my hair in a ponytail, sprayed some body mist, and called it a day. As soon as I was ready to walk out of my bedroom, Sky stood in front of the door.

"Did you and Pops have sex?" she said with a smirk, batting her eyebrows.

"No, creep," I laughed. "Why do you even want to know if your mother and father have sex?"

"Because I miss my mother and my father. I'm just wondering if they miss each other," she said. I rolled my eyes because she was so damn nosey. But she was my best friend, and with her baby face, it didn't even seem like she was 26.

"I'll be back, child. Just let me go see what Jerry is doing in my kitchen, and we'll talk."

I ran downstairs.

"Beautiful," he called me.

"Hey, chef," I replied as he walked over and kissed me.

"I hope you're hungry. I'm cooking up something special for you. Will your daughter be joining us?"

"I thank you for doing this for me. I really appreciate it. I will ask her. In the meantime, do you need my help with anything? Or do you need me to find something for you?"

"No, I'm good. Go do what you need to do."

"Okay, I'll be back shortly."

I headed back upstairs to talk with Sky. I told her that we had a great time last night with the kids. It really took me back to old times. I told her we kissed and that I told him I was now dating. I let her know that I still loved Sean a lot, but his situation didn't sit right with me. In order to keep my peace, I couldn't be in that space.

"It was one thing when he cheated, and I took him back. I won't forget, but I was willing to forgive, move past it, and work on being better for each other. It was another thing when there was now a child who was the product of that encounter. Now, it was always going to be in my face. I would always reminded that my husband was inside another woman. My husband created a bond with that woman that will last the rest of their lives because they have that child. I hated it when people said it was *only* 18 years—no, it's a lifetime. There are college graduations, marriages, baby showers, and life-making events. Their bond is forever. *That* is why I ended it. I couldn't deal with it. The hurt I felt every time the baby was here, every time he went to her house, trying to be strong and not worry about what could happen. Every time she called or texted, I was always unsure, and the pain became unbearable."

"Damn, Mom. Wow! I never knew you felt that way. You said you had a good time last night? Did you still feel that way being around Fatts?"

"She wasn't there. Sean said she was sick. It was a good night because my family was together. Don't get me wrong, Fatts is the sweetest, most beautiful little girl. It's not her fault she didn't ask to be here, but that's also another reason. How can I accept her as one of my own, as a part of my family, if I feel this way when I see her? It's way different from Lil Sean. When he came around, everything just fit perfectly. He felt like my child from the gate. Stepmom was never my title; it was always 'mom.' But with her, it doesn't feel that way. It's like my heart won't let me accept her. So, I think it's best that we go our own ways."

"Do you think that will ever change? That one day you may feel differently?" Sky asked.

"Baby, I couldn't tell you anything about the future. All I know is, right now, it hasn't changed."

My phone rang.

"Hey, beautiful. Food's done. I made your daughter a plate, too, just in case," Jerry said.

"Thank you. Coming down now," I replied before hanging up the phone.

"Jerry made you a plate. Are you going to join us?" I asked Sky.

"I guess if he's going to be in your life, I've got to get to know him. But if the food is trash, I'm leaving. You're on your own."

I laughed. "Deal," she said as she shook my hand before we headed downstairs.

After the kids opened all their gifts and got dressed on Christmas morning, I took them to their dad's house. The kids were so excited when we walked in because everyone was there—his friends, Mally, James, my friend Lay, Tiff, Ebony, Kelly, Kenny, Uncle Joe, and Jo'el. They were all eating breakfast, laughing, and having a good time. Everyone was just in such good spirits. I'm not going to lie; I missed being around this group. Oh, and his baby's mom was there.

"Tiera!" Mally screamed my name as I walked in the door and came over to hug me. Everyone else followed. They all told me they missed me and asked if I was staying.

I greeted everyone, even Fatts and Megan. I was glad they were on their way out as I was coming in. I didn't want the awkwardness.

I handed Sean the gift I got for him and the gift I also got for Fatts from the kids.

"Thank you, I appreciate you," he said, standing beside her while holding their baby. I just smiled and nodded.

"Hey, where's Sky?" he asked.

"She just called me; she's on her way," I said as I handed Joe Jo'el's gift.

I wanted to at least make my way around to everyone before I left, starting with my God baby. I took her right out of Joe's arms.

"Oh, my, you're getting so big now, looking just like your mommy. Hi, my love," I said to her and gave her lots of kisses.

Sean told the kids to wait to open their gifts while he walked his little family to the car.

"Ok. She left. You can talk shit about her now, Tiera. We're all here for it." Mally said, and I laughed as everyone told him to shut up.

"I'm okay, Mally, thank you."

"T, come on and get some of this food, girl," Kelly said.

"No, thank you, boo. I'm about to leave," I said as Sean walked back in.

"She's gotta go be with her new boyfriend," he said to everyone.

I just stared at him and asked, "Why?" Confused as to why he would even bring that up in front of everyone, especially with our children in the next room.

"You are, though, aren't you?" he asked.

"You're still sleeping with your baby mom, right?" I replied.

I heard Tiff say, "Oop," and Joe choked on his drink. He stood there, looked at me, and shook his head, saying, "Nah."

"Whatever, Sean." I gave the baby back to Joe. "Bye, everyone. It was great seeing you all. Lay, call me later. Merry Christmas, everyone; bye, children."

"What about your gifts? You really not gonna take the time out to open them?" Sean asked, standing there, just looking at me.

"I'll get them when I pick the kids up. I have to go."

"Do you?" he asked softly as he opened the door for me.

I looked back at him. "Yes, Sean, I do," I said and closed the door. [▶ "All I Have" by AMERIE]

The next few months with Jerry were great. We met at my company's networking meet-and-greet party about two months after Sean left the house. Two months after that, we started dating. He was the CEO of Collaborated Culture, Inc., a high-end clothing line. The socks alone were $150. He was two years older than me and had a son who was in college. He wasn't all that tall; we were around the same height, but it worked. He was light-skinned with big, beautiful green eyes, and he was mixed with black and white. He was a phenomenal dresser. In a suit, he was GQ magazine sharp, but outside of work, not so much. If I had to put a face to him, I would say he reminded me of the dad from that old TV show *Smart Guy*, just with green eyes—the same kind of outfits and everything. He was just a regular guy. I think that's what I liked the most about him. Plus, the man could cook. I mean, like top chef-type cooking. Sometimes, I just sat in the kitchen with him, drank my wine, and watched him cook. I loved the time we spent together. He never made me feel bad about always working. In fact, he motivated me to be better. We hadn't done anything sexual yet, and he didn't rush me, which I thought was sexy.

As for me and Sean, if it wasn't about the kids, we didn't speak. He was living his life, and I was living mine. I started working a hybrid schedule for the kids, so we rarely ever saw each other at work, and when we did, it was just a "hey," if that. After I told him I was dating, it seemed like he lost all interest in me. When

I dropped off the kids, I stayed in the car, as did he. I felt some way for a while, but being with Jerry helped me let the feelings go. I was happy. [▶ **"Beautiful" by INDIA. ARIE**]

Six Months Later...

"Good morning, ladies," Tracey said as she opened the door and stuck her head into our office.

"Good morning, Tracey," a few of us replied.

"Hey, Tiera, when you get a chance, come up to my office. We need to talk."

"Sure, let me put these documents on my desk and I'll be right up," I assured her.

"Great!" she said, waving to Nola as she left.

I scurried into my office and threw the files on my desk. For Tracey to come all the way downstairs and tell me personally that she had something to tell me, it must have been important. Once upstairs and in her office, she told me to close the door and have a seat. She leaned back in her chair, crossed her arms, and smiled. I crossed my legs and sat back in my chair. *Oh yeah, this was about to be good,* I thought to myself, wondering what company gossip she had for today.

"I'm retiring." She said, leaning forward over her desk. She smiled as if she were telling me something good.

"What? No! You can't!" I said, shocked.

"My husband talked us into buying a boat this weekend."

"A boat?"

"Yes, a boat," she smiled with excitement. "We went to one of his friend's parties on this extravagant yacht in Ocean City, Maryland, and it was absolutely amazing. The next day, we both agreed to go look at boats for ourselves. Long story short, I've decided that 35 years of my time is all I'm willing to give to this company. I want to wake up early in the morning and go have breakfast on my boat with my husband while watching the sunrise while I'm still able to do it."

"I completely understand that, and that sounds amazing. Who have you told?" I asked.

"Just you. Because in 20 minutes, we will meet with Ryan, and I will announce my retirement and my replacement... *You!*"

I put my hand over my chest. "*Me?*"

"Yes, you. There is no one more qualified for the job. You're my right hand—hell, sometimes I'm your right hand. You learned faster than I did when I started out. Let's be honest here, Tiera. You're efficient at your job and mine."

"I don't know what to say," I replied, feeling overjoyed, excited, and overwhelmed simultaneously.

She sat back in her chair and rocked. "Ten percent required travel to your current 75 percent. Major increase in salary. More time to be home with your wonderful children. Impressive PTO package. The arduous work you've put in is over. Now you just coast and enforce until retirement. It took me 15 years to do and learn what you have in, what, five or six years? If you want the job, I'll make sure it's yours."

"Of course I want it. YES! I'm just taken aback by all of this. WOW! Are you moving Keshia up to my position?"

"Absolutely not." We both laughed. "We're going external for your position. Shit, you should maybe think about replacing her in your old position. I'm just saying. But I'll leave that up to you."

The phone rang.

"Hello?" Tracey answered.

"Okay, tell him we're coming now. Thank you, Gloria," she said before hanging up. "Ryan is here. Are you ready?"

I smiled. "I'm always ready!"

Once I was out of the meeting, tears just started falling. All I could say was, "Thank you, God!" Everything I had worked so hard for had come to pass. At the beginning of the new year, I would be the new VP of Best Trucking. I pulled out my phone, stepped outside, and called Jerry.

"Beautiful," he greeted.

"I made VP!"

"VP of what, beautiful?"

"Um, my company," I said, confused.

"That's nice, honey. Look, can we talk about this over dinner tonight? I'm really busy."

"Oh, okay, sure. No problem."

Jerry hung up.

Huh. I saw that conversation going differently in my head. I thought he would indulge in my joy and excitement with me. Disappointed and embarrassed, I just went back inside.

Later that night, Jerry picked me up from my house. When I opened the door, he was holding a huge bouquet of long-stemmed roses—at least 40 or 60 roses.

"Congrats, love," he said, leaning in and kissing me on the cheek.

"Thank you! These are beautiful, Jerry!" I took the roses inside and set them on the countertop.

"Hey, I hope you don't mind, but I invited a few of my friends out to dinner with us," he said.

"No, not at all," I replied as I walked out and closed the door behind us.

Inside the restaurant, we walked over to the table where his friends were. Jerry introduced me to his friends Kanwal, Rodney, and Rodney's wife, Mary Anne.

"I hope you don't mind. I ordered a bottle of Prosecco for the table," Kanwal added. Prosecco was Jerry's favorite.

"Not at all, my brother, not at all," Jerry said with excitement. Rodney was the only "brother" I saw at the table, but I kept my thoughts to myself. He pulled out my chair for me. The restaurant was very upscale. It was located in the downtown area of Philadelphia, Rittenhouse Square, I believe. The servers wore all-black suits, black shirts, and white gloves. It just felt like a place where people came to do business, make deals, and buy multi-million-dollar homes or boats like Tracey's. I could get used to this. The food was simply amazing. Jerry requested that the chef come out and meet with us so we could sing his praises for the delicious food. The chef was so appreciative and grateful for the $500 tip that Jerry, Kanwal, and Rodney gave him that he made us his signature dessert, which wasn't even on the menu. The whole night was top-tier. As the new VP, I felt like this was somewhere I belonged. Well, that's what I thought at first.

As the night went on, Jerry and his friends went through four bottles of wine and a few glasses of scotch. Their normal conversations turned arrogant, and they all wreaked of entitlement.

"Tiera, I hear you're the new VP of a delivery service," Rodney said nonchalantly, as if I wasn't the VP of one of the top five trucking services in the country.

"Yes, VP of Best Trucking," I proclaimed.

"Woah," he said, shocked. "Best Trucking is an elite corporation there, Ms. Lady. Good for you." Rodney said, hitting Jerry on the arm.

"Best Trucking, FedEx, UPS—all the same, am I right?" Jerry asked the table and laughed. It felt like my job was some little thing to him.

"Well, congratulations," Mary Anne said.

"Thank you."

"Yes, yes, congrats, beautiful," Jerry said, drunk, raising his glass. "Now you can fire your delivery driver, baby daddy." He laughed again and continued, "You won't be needing his little child support checks anymore." Then, he high-fived Kanwal.

"First off, he's my ex-husband, not my baby daddy. I do not receive child support checks, nor have I ever needed them. And he's an excellent father, by the way." I moved closer to him. "I think you need to ease up on the drinks there, buddy. I'm going to the bathroom. When I get back, I'll be ready to leave."

I excused myself from the table and walked outside. I was so upset but mainly disappointed. I had never seen this side of him. Sean would never display himself in that manner, especially in front of people. He was so quick to always want to speak ill of Sean when he didn't even know him. I was ready to go.

After I took a breather, I went back in and got the keys from Jerry because he was not driving me home drunk. I told everyone goodnight and safe travels, and then we left. On the drive home, I wanted to talk to Jerry about his actions, but he went to sleep. This was probably for the best—I was upset, and he wasn't in the right mindset to handle this conversation.

When we got back to my house, I made him get out of the car and guided him to the couch, where he could sleep off the rest of his bullshit. I wasn't going to let him drive home in this state. I went upstairs, got undressed, laid in bed, and called an old friend. [▶ **"Thinking About Me" by DVSN**]

Sean: Yeah, Tiera.

He answered in a *very* dry tone.

Me: I made VP.
Sean: Oh shit... are you serious?

In an instant, his new tone evoked the same level of excitement I had when I found out I got the job.

Me: Yes.
Sean: Shit, Tiera, this is big—like, *major.*
Me: I know, right? That's what I've been feeling since I got out of the meeting with Tracey and Ryan.
Sean: Ryan Goldbyrd? The President?
Me: Yes.
Sean: Damn girl, you made it! Aw man, I'm so very proud of you. You deserve it. I'm happy for you.

Him rooting for me like that gave me butterflies. The feeling he gave me was like a double dose of dopamine running throughout my whole body.

Me: Thank you, Sean. That means so much to me, hearing you say that.

Sean: Of course. I've seen the long nights and how hard you've worked.

I began to tear up. It was the reaction I'd longed for all day.

Me: So, what's been going on with you? We haven't talked in a very long time.

Sean: I know. Well, I'm not a VP or anything, but I bought a bobtail truck. Nothing fancy. I got a great deal from another trucking company that was going out of business. I started doing my own deliveries after work during the weeks I don't have the kids. I pick up trailers and drop them off. I've got five clients so far. Something small.

Me: Oh my god, Sean, now that's major! Boy, forget VP—you're the CEO of your own business. There's nothing small about that. Do you have a name for your business yet?

Sean: Of course. It's Twin Trucking. Hopefully, it will grow, and maybe one day I can leave Best. I do a couple hundred every other week, shit, $3200 when I went out to Yonkers, but I need the benefits and insurance—that's the only thing that's keeping me there.

Me: Aww, Sean. Yeah, I love the name. It's perfect. You know I can put you on my benefits if you want. We're not divorced yet. You should go after your dreams. I told you years ago to put Lil' Sean on my benefits around the time the twins were born.

Sean: Thanks, but I'll work it out.

He laughed.

Sean: But thanks for telling me. So, Mrs. VP, how does it feel to get everything you wanted?

Me: Well, I don't have everything...

Sean began having a background conversation with Meg, which annoyed me.

Me: It's getting late, so I'm going to let you go. And again, congratulations.

Sean: Thank you, and same to you, Mrs. VP.

Me: Goodnight, Sean.

Sean: Goodnight, Tiera.

Before he was my husband, he was my best friend. A part of me missed that friendship.

The next morning, the sound of knocking on the door woke me up. "Come in," I said.

"Hey, beautiful," Jerry said as he entered my room. I'd forgotten he was even here. Still disgusted by his actions last night, his sweet remarks weren't going to cut it.

"Thank you for letting me stay last night. I don't even remember coming back here," he laughed. "I think I should cut back."

"Yeah, you should," I replied, sitting up in bed. He came over and sat at the bottom of the bed.

"Sorry if my friends seemed stuck up. That's just how they are."

"No, that's how *you* all are, and I don't think that's a good reason to be stuck up."

"Me? Stuck up?" he asked, then laughed. "Did you not have a good time?"

"At first, I did, yes. I was having a great time, but you showed me a side of you that I was not impressed with. Not only did you belittle my ex-husband, but you also discredited my promotion in front of your friends. I don't know these people, so don't go sharing my life with them. My business is my business to tell, not yours. They didn't need to know I have an ex-husband or that he works with me, nor the bullshit about him paying child support. I never even told you that. So from now on, don't discuss me in front of anyone. And I will not be going out with your friends again. And if you don't know how to control your drinking, I will not be going out with you either."

He looked at me, stunned and perplexed.

"Are we on the same page now?" I asked.

"Yeah, you're right, and I'm sorry, love. I got carried away. Please forgive me. I didn't mean to embarrass you. I will never let that happen again." He kissed my hand and looked up at me with those beautiful green eyes. "Can I make you some breakfast?" he smiled. I agreed, only because I was hungry, and he could cook, but I was still pissed.

Two weeks passed, and Sean and I talked a lot more than usual. I felt like we were becoming closer friends. When we talked or texted, it wasn't just about the kids anymore. We laughed, joked, and shared memes and photos. I must say, I enjoyed it.

Today was Lil' Sean's 14th birthday party. Sean and I went half on a party for him at his favorite place, Lightning Strike. There were go-karts, laser tag, ax-throwing—basically everything. The party cost us $1200 for 25 people, and that didn't even include a cake or pizza—just access to play and free drinks. It was a surprise party, so Sean dropped off the cake and then picked up Lil' Sean. He thought his dad was taking him shopping and to get a haircut for his actual birthday on Wednesday. I had my mom pick up the twins because God forbid, Sean only takes one of them and not the others. The twins would have a fit, and I couldn't tell them anything because they tell *everything*. Those two couldn't hold water.

Sean called me and told me he was outside, so I unlocked my car so he could put the cake in there. When he was done, I let Lil' Sean know his dad was here.

"Bye, Mom," he said, running out to the car and getting in.

When I walked outside and over to the car, he just backed out of the driveway. There was no hello, no small talk. It was bizarre because we'd been texting all morning. He was acting like an estranged baby daddy just picking up our kid.

I tried not to dwell on it too much. I went back into the house, retrieved all the party supplies from my room closet, and called to order the pizzas for Sky to pick up. After loading the back seat of my car, I got into the driver's seat and noticed Jerry's shoes had been tossed into the front. They must have been in the trunk where Sean had placed the cake, and he must have thrown them to the front. I began to wonder if this was the reason for his sudden change in attitude. *Was he upset*? I'd never considered him to be the type to get jealous.

When I got to the place, Lay and James were already there to help set everything up. Then Mom came with the twins, followed by Sky and her boyfriend. I was so glad that there was a lot of helping hands because I didn't realize how much stuff had to be done once we got there. There was so little time. We only had four hours, and we needed at least an hour to set up.

While we were working, people started arriving. I had my mom stand at the door to be on the lookout for Sean. I finally got the cake on the table, and my mom yelled, "Here they come!"

When Lil Sean walked in and saw everyone, he was so surprised. He smiled from ear to ear. He hugged his dad, then ran over and hugged me. When I kissed him, he became emotional and hugged me again. He hadn't really wanted a birthday party since his aunt passed, so this was very special for him. It only took five minutes, and then he and his friends ran off to play.

"Did you see how happy he was?" I smiled and watched him and his friends run over to the go-karts. "We did good," I said to Sean, touching his back.

"Yeah," he said quickly, moving away from me and walking off to talk to his friends. He didn't even look my way. I decided that this was not what was going to happen—not today. He wasn't going to act like I didn't exist and make this day awkward, so I kindly grabbed his arm and pulled him to the side.

"I get it. You saw the shoes in my trunk. Sean, we went to the gym one morning, and he left them in my car," I said.

He tried to flag me off and walk away, but I wasn't letting that happen. "Talk to me," I said.

"Why is that man's shoes in your car, Tiera? So, you got my kids just playing over top of another man's shoes?"

"Sean, what? Playing over his shoes? As if they were crack pipes? They were in the trunk. And we are dating, so yes, his things may be in my car occasionally."

"So, what are you texting and calling me for?" He asked.

"I thought we were friends. I thought we were slowly moving past what we've been through these past 10 months. Are we not? Plus, I never said I wasn't dating him."

"But you're kikiing with me on the phone while letting another man leave his shoes in your car?"

"And you're still doing whatever you're doing. As you should, since we're not together. Is this really about shoes, Sean? The same way you feel about another man's shoes being in my car is the same way I felt when I found out your seed was in another woman's stomach—multiplied by 100! Don't act like you don't know the reason why we're here in the first place," I added, and I walked off just as Megan walked in to drop off their daughter.

About an hour later, I could tell that he knew he was in the wrong because he started being his playful, goofy self again. He bumped me a few times and made some jokes. It was his own way of saying he was sorry without actually saying it. He was acting like a Black mom asking you if you're hungry after she beat you. I just let bygones be bygones. We got in the go-karts with the twins. We even took Fatts and Jo'el into the ball pit. This day wasn't about us and our feelings; it was about coming together as parents to celebrate our son's birthday. After the cake and the gifts, it seemed like four hours flew by. Everyone enjoyed themselves. There was a lot of laughter and many memories made. It was good to see the crew again and to hang out with everyone. It was a good day. Our son is very loved, and he had the gifts to prove it.

As I was packing up the car, Sean came over to me.

"Hey, umm, I just want to apologize for the way I was acting. I let my feelings get the best of me. You're right, you are dating him, and where his shoes are is none of my business."

"Thank you, Sean. I appreciate that."

"Just do me one favor," he asked.

"What's that?"

"Just let me meet him before you let him meet the kids."

"Of course, Sean. I would love that."

"Hey, Dad!" Lil Sean screamed and ran up to us as we stood outside of the car. "Can you come to the house and play my new game with me and Oliver?"

"Why don't you and Oliver come to *my* house?" Sean told him.

"In the hood?" he whispered. Sean and I both bust out laughing.

"Boy, what you mean in the hood? It is, in fact, not the hood. You grew up in that house."

"It's okay for me, Dad, but..." he pulled Sean down to him. "He's *white*."

"Hey, if it's good enough for you, it's good enough for him. White people be in the hood too."

"Dad, you know what I mean."

"T, do you mind?" he asked me.

"No, I was going out anyway, and Sky was going to watch them, but I can tell Sky to go on about her day."

"Yeah, I'll watch them."

Lil Sean screamed over to Oliver. "Yo, O, we good? Let's go!" and they hopped in the car.

"When did he become so uppity?" we laughed. "The hood? That boy don't know one thing about the hood, acting like I live on Kensington Ave," he said.

"Hey, y'all!" Tiff ran up to us. "Soooo, guys, where's the after-party gonna be? This can't be it. It's been a while since everyone has been together, and Kelly leaves tomorrow."

"My house," I quickly responded, not even sure why.

"Okay, cool. Can Sean come?" She pointed to him and laughed. He put her in a headlock and laughed.

"I guess he can come," I said.

"Okay, okay, I was just making sure. I'm gonna run and grab some chicken and something else. Do y'all want anything? Matter of fact... Aye yo, James and Mal, after-party at Tiera's house. I'm going to run and get some chicken from ACME," she yelled.

"Oh word? Lay and I gon' run to Roger Wilco then and grab some bottles."

"Hold up!" Mal yelled. "Aye, Tiera, can Sean come over too?"

They all bust out laughing. Sean put his middle finger up at them.

Tiff screamed out, "MazeTown!" as she ran off to her car.

"I guess I'll see you at the house?"

"Yeah," he said as he turned and walked to his car.

It felt like everything was back to normal with his friends, my mom, all the kids around. I started having so much fun hosting this after-party with Sean as if we were together again. They didn't even end up playing the game. All the kids ended up in the pool. Joe even put Fatts and Jo'el in the twins' old floating chairs. All the kids were outside, and the adults were inside, listening to the oldies, eating chicken, and having drinks. Mom put her favorite song on, "Signed, Sealed, delivered" by Stevie Wonder, and started to do her little dance. Next thing you know, she had everyone bopping like we were all 60-plus years old. She played The Temptations, The Supremes, The Dells, and The O'Jays. If it had "The" in the front of the name, she played it. One by one, she had everyone dancing. Kelly and her boyfriend danced, Mom danced with Mally, and Tiff and her girlfriend danced. It wasn't until Mom put on "I Second That Emotion" by Smokey Robinson that Sean asked me to dance, and of course, I danced with him. It was an instant yes! We used to dance all the time, just the two of us, right there in the living room. I guess you could say it was our thing. It was like we fell right back to where we used to be. For a long time, things between us had been awkward whenever we were around each other. But today, we just let ourselves be ourselves. After dancing, we both leaned back on the countertop in the kitchen. He put his arm around my shoulders.

I leaned over into his shirt.

"You smell good. Is that new?" I asked.

"Thank you. Yeah, Kelly got it for me from Paris for my birthday."

"It works for you."

Sky walked past as we were having small talk.

"What's this?" She asked, pointing at us, smiling, and raising her eyebrows.

"What? We're friends," I said.

"Don't forget parents," he added.

"Yes, parents, who are friends," I rephrased.

"Umm-hmm. Well, if it means anything, this is the happiest I've seen both of you in a very long time," she shrugged. "I'm just saying," and she walked away.

We both looked at each other and then my eyes caught the time on the stove. I almost forgot I was going out.

"I've got to go," I said to him.

"Okay." He took his arm from around me and headed over to his friends. I quickly got dressed and told Jerry not to pick me up. It would have been a bad idea; could you imagine him showing up to pick me up with Sean and all his friends here? They would've eaten him alive. I told him I would meet him. As I said goodbyes, they begged me to stay. I really wanted to, but I couldn't. Sean came up to me and whispered in my ear.

"He's a lucky man." I smiled and looked into his eyes.

"So are you! Because I'm raising your children."

"That you are," he said as he backed up and raised his beer to me.

"Kiss her already!" Joe yelled, which started a "Kiss her!" chant. We both smiled and made googly eyes at each other, but we didn't kiss. Deep down, I wished he would've grabbed me and kissed me. But he didn't.

"Have fun, everyone," I said, grabbing my purse off the table.

[▶ "Good Good" by USHER]

You ever feel like you're in the right place, at the right time, just with the wrong person? That's how I felt the whole night with Jerry. Everything was great. He took me out on a boat ride, where we had a candlelit dinner while watching the sunset. He was such a gentleman, I almost forgot about what happened a few weeks ago while dining with his friends. After dinner, they brought out dessert, which was delightful. He took me down to the cabin, to a room with two massage tables for us to get a massage. After the massage therapists left, it was just me and him. He fed me strawberries and gave me an extended massage. Then he kissed me and said, "I want to taste you." So, I let him right there on the table. I must say, he was getting better at it. Of course, one thing led to another, and we ended up having sex. He worked me up and got me in the mood, but sex with Jerry was not my favorite. He was long and pointy, like a pencil. There was no girth, and it felt like he was just stabbing my cervix. He loved it, though. The man came in 10 minutes. Thank God, because there was no pleasure for me. The few times we had sex, I did it only for him. Faking it became easy. Other than that, tonight was absolutely everything.

"I had a wonderful night, beautiful. Did you enjoy yourself?" he said as we walked off the boat, holding hands.

"Yes, thank you so much. I had a wonderful time. You always make me feel special."

"Maybe we can keep enjoying ourselves regularly, if you know what I mean." He raised an eyebrow.

"Um, maybe," I said, though I was thinking *That's not going to happen any time soon.*

He laughed. "No rush. I know you have kids."

"Yes, I do. Thank you for understanding."

He walked me to my car and opened the door for me. He leaned in and kissed me.

"Call me when you get home. Let me know you got in safe."

"Of course." He closed my door, and I drove off.

The night was great, but the best part was driving back, pulling up to my house, and seeing that big-ass Jeep in my driveway. Now, that made my heart smile.

When I got inside, Sean was watching TV on the couch.

"How was your night?" he asked, turning down the TV.

"It was nice. And yours?" I said, knowing damn well he didn't want to hear about my night.
He stood up and stretched.

"It was great. Your children thought they were going to pull an all-nighter, but I made them go to bed at nine."

"I bet. That many people haven't been here in a while. Their excitement level was probably on 1000. What time did everyone leave?"

"Your mom left after I put the twins down. Everyone else stayed until about 11. Sky helped me clean up, and then she took off. But I'm gonna go get Fatts so we can leave—it's late."

"Yes, it's late. Just stay. I'm sure the kids will be happy to wake up and see that you're here."

"You sure?"

"Yeah."

"Okay, cool. Thanks."

"Don't do that. We're still family. You don't have to thank me. Sleep well. Goodnight." I said, walking over to the steps.

"Goodnight."

I went upstairs, blushing. As soon as I got upstairs, I made a plan in my head. I was going to take a quick shower, put on some night clothes, call Jerry to tell him I made it home safe, take some blankets downstairs to Sean, and maybe watch a movie or two with him. As I was changing and talking to Jerry, Sean burst into my room and closed the door behind him.

I told Jerry I'd call him back and hung up quickly.

"Sean, what are you doing? This is no longer your room. You can't just bust in without knocking."

He walked up to me and tried to kiss me, but I moved away and pushed his face back. Not because I didn't want him to, but because I had just been kissing and having sex with another man. I grabbed my shirt and covered myself since I was half-naked.

"That's crazy. And please," He waved me off. "I've seen way more than that. Yo, I don't want you seeing him anymore."

"Excuse me?"

"You heard me. I don't want you seeing him, dating him, or having any contact with him anymore," he said, as Jerry continued to call me back-to-back.

"Wait, so you think you can just bust into my room and dictate my life? Is there a reason why I shouldn't see him, Sean?"

"Yo, do you love him?"

"What?" I said, confused.

"Man, I don't even care. Listen, I don't want him around my kids, this house, or you. You understand?"

"Do I understand? Woah… And again, what is your reason?"

I was thinking he might say something like, *because I love you, because I want my family back,* or any good reason, like, *I want my marriage to work.* No. Instead, he said, "Because I said so."

Everything I had been feeling before he walked in disappeared in an instant. He completely changed my attitude. I didn't know which one of his friends hyped him up tonight, but his audacity was at its peak.

"I think it's best you leave, Sean."

"You got it," he said and walked out.

I wanted to scream, because if he would've just stayed his ass downstairs without coming up here making demands, shit, who knows what it could've led to.

I answered the phone.

"Sorry, sorry. Sean just busted in my room."

"Your ex?"

"Yes."

"Why is he at your house?"

"Lil Sean wanted him to come over and play his new game with him."

"Why couldn't he take his son to his house?"

"Our son? And why does it matter where he watches his children? Especially if I'm with you."

"He shouldn't be there, and if we're going to be together, I don't want him there inside your house. Come on, Tiera, how is that fair to me? It's 2 a.m., and my girl's ex-husband is at her house."

"Goddamn! Men and their demands," I said as I watched Sean back out of my driveway and pull off from my bedroom window. "Only Tiera tells Tiera what to do, and you both have fucked up a great evening. Have a good night, Jerry," I said and hung up again.

Four days went by, and I hadn't talked to Jerry or Sean. Jerry had been away on business, and Sean only texted me once to tell me to have the kids ready Saturday so he could pick them up for Fatts' birthday party. My mother told me I needed to take some time for myself. She said if I didn't know what to do, not to do anything at all, and that's what I had been doing all week.

Tonight, I told the kids that we could order whatever they wanted because I wasn't cooking. As they were looking over menus, trying to come to one decision, someone rang the doorbell. When I opened it, it was Jerry holding flowers. I stepped outside and closed the door.

"What are you doing here? You can't just come by my house unannounced. My children are here."

"I couldn't wait another day to see you."

"You could have FaceTimed me. Don't just show up at my house. I thought we went over that."

"I'm sorry, my love, but..."

"Mommy, who is it?"

I heard TT's voice behind me as she opened the door. Next thing you know, Taj and Lil Sean were at the door too.

"Is this your boyfriend, mom?" Taj asked.

"Ye—" Jerry began to speak, but I cut him off.

"No, this is Mr. Jerry, my friend from work. Say hello, since you want to be so nosey." They all greeted him, and he greeted them back. "And who told you I have a boyfriend?"

"The streets, mommy, the streets," Taj said, flexing his little chest.

"The streets, huh?" I laughed. "Okay, cool guy. Well, go back inside and find out what the house has to say."

Lil Sean pulled both of them back inside and told them to go find something to order.

I turned back to Jerry. "That's exactly what I didn't want to happen. I promised their father you'd meet him before they did," I whispered to Jerry.

"Thank you," I said to Lil Sean. Instead of closing the door and leaving me and Jerry alone, he stepped back out the door and closed the door behind him so now it was the was the three of us.

"So, *you're* the guy that's been giving my mom all these flowers?" he asked Jerry with much confidence.

Jerry laughed. "Um…" He cleared his throat. "Yes, yes, sir, that's me. And you must be Lil…"

"You can call me SJ," he said, feeling himself. "She deserves it, so you should keep buying them. But her favorite is sunflowers."

"Is that so?" Jerry replied. Lil Sean nodded.

"I can't thank you enough for the advice, SJ."

"You're welcome." He reached his hand out for the flowers Jerry had for me. "I'll put them in some water for her," he added as he took the flowers from Jerry and walked back inside the house.

I was utterly blown away. *Not my son confronting a man over me. Not him going by the name SJ. My son was growing up so fast*, I thought to myself.

"I think I like SJ! He's smooth and assertive," Jerry laughed.

"He sure is."

"Now, if you let me come in, I can just cook for everyone, and you won't have to order?"

"No."

"Fine. Can I pick you up tomorrow? We added a new Collaborated Culture store to the mall, and I want to go check it out. Then we can go have dinner." He took my hand and looked at me with those beautiful eyes. They were hypnotizing. I smiled.

"Okay, sure." I pulled my hand out for a handshake. I didn't want him to try and be affectionate in case the kids popped up at any time. "I'll have my mom pick up the kids."

He chuckled and shook my hand. "I get it. Great! Later, beautiful."

SMOLDER

Sean

Chapter Playlist

▶ POST MALONE, MARK MORRISON & SICK-ICK—"Cooped Up/ Return of The Mack"

▶ ASHANTI—"Breakup 2 Makeup"

▶ TREY SONGZ & TI—"2 Reasons"

▶ OMARION—"I'm Sayin"

▶ USHER—"Good Kisser"

▶ OMARION—"Post To Be"

▶ J. HOLIDAY—"Yours"

▶ CHRIS BROWN—"Privacy"

▶ DANIEL CAESAR & BRANDY—"Love Again"

▶ DVSN—"Hallucinations"

▶ P.M. DAWN —"I'd Die Without You"

When I got home, Meg called and told me what she needed for Fatt's birthday party. My baby was turning two tomorrow. So, I suggested we meet up at the mall since I had to go there, anyway. She said that would be perfect since she needed to get Fatt's ears pierced for the party. Just like I was there to hold TT while she got hers pierced, I wanted to hold my other daughter as well. We met up at the mall and got everything we needed for the party. It had been about a week since I saw my baby, so I was very happy to spend some time with her. Just like TT, she was a champ. She jumped but didn't cry a single tear. I would never miss out on a moment like this with any one of my children, no matter what.

After we got her ears done, we got a bite to eat at the food court and just vibed out for a while. A while back, after I left the house with T and the kids, Meg and I tried to do the whole family thing, but it just didn't feel right for either of us. We came to the realization that we were using each other for sex at that point. We were lonely. I was still in love with T, and she was still in love with her ex-husband. So, that whole thing was very short-lived. If I had to say, it lasted only about a month or two. After that, we just co-parented. She was also like one of my friends, just like Kelly or Tiff.

It's crazy how you see your life going, and then it completely turns around and becomes something else. They say if you want to make God laugh, tell him your plans. I bet my G was up there in tears from laughing at my plans.

As we were leaving the mall, I was rolling Fatt's stroller, and Meg was right beside me eating a pretzel. I didn't know whose name should be Fatts, hers or our baby's, but that was another story. As we were walking back to our cars, guess who we ran into? T and some dorky dude. This must've been her nigga. She saw me, and I saw her. I stopped the stroller as we were about to pass each other and spoke.

"What's up, T?" I said, playing it cool but pissed off and hurt at the same time. I hadn't seen her up close and in person since the night of Lil Sean's birthday party.

She really out here with another dude for the world to see? I know it's been almost a year, but we're not even divorced yet, I thought to myself, along with other thoughts like, *She better not have this dude around my kids.* Her eyes hit all three of us. She looked at the baby, Meg, and me before saying anything.

"Hey, Sean…" she paused. "Megan."

Meg waved and said "Hey, girl."

"This is Jerry. Jerry, this is Megan, my ex-husband, and their baby," T continued.

Jerry looked at her, then back at me, and held out his hand for a handshake. I wasn't going to be petty today, so I shook his hand and nodded.

"Hey man, nice to meet you. Your kids are great," he said with a smile.

"My kids, huh?" I looked at T with a straight face, but I knew she could read my eyes, saying, *Why the fuck has he been around my kids?* I told her I wanted to meet him first. T looked down, knowing she was wrong.

"Well, we have to go," she insisted. "What time are you picking up the twins tomorrow? I don't think Lil Sean wants to go." She stumbled over her words at the end.

"Why doesn't he want to go?" I asked, confused.

"You know he's 14 now. All he wants to do is play that game. He even asked if we could start calling him SJ. I don't know. Call him and ask him," she said as she walked away, grabbing Jerry's arm and cutting the conversation short. [▶ **"Breakup 2 Makeup" by ASHANTI**]

I forgot Meg was there for a moment. It was awkward, but she was eating her pretzel and in her own little world. I looked at her as we walked on. I pushed the stroller to the car and put Fatts in the car seat. I kissed my baby on her forehead and told her I loved her before closing the door.

Before I walked off to hop in my car, Meg grabbed me and said, "Sean, I know we both messed up, but you never allowed that to come between you and your daughter. I thank you."

I nodded and hugged her. She told me only time would tell—maybe my relationship still had a chance.

"I have hope for you because I know there's no hope for me," she said, referring to her getting back with her husband.

"Only time will tell," I said gruffly as I walked off. "Get home safe," I yelled back.

Once in the car, my mind was racing. *My wife really had a boyfriend and had my kids around him. What the fuck is going on? Does she love him?* At that moment, feeling defeated, I got a text message from my co-worker.

Mack

Today 7:00 PM

Mack

> Yo…Big man, what you doing tonight? the gang heading out to Brit's party you trying to run through.

Now, some may know Brit, and some may not. Let's just say it was an old story, but tonight might be a new chapter. Fuck it. My wife is moving on, so why shouldn't I?

Me

> Drop me the info and ill slide.

Mack sent the info, and now all I needed was the sidekick. I called up Mal; he was always down for anything with drinks and women.

Mally: Sup, limp dick.
Me: You trying to roll with me to this party tonight?
Mally: Who's party?

Me: Remember the young jawn I used to kick it with way back when, B?

Mally: The Jawn that swallowed most of your kids with the thick ass glasses?

I laughed.

Me: Bro, you stupid. But yeah, that's her. Are you in?

Mally: Wait, isn't T like her boss?

Me: Yeah.

Mally: Nigga, that shit messy...

He paused for a second.

Mally: Alright, text me the info. I'm in. My nigga is back in the game. Good for you, my boy!! WHOOO-HOO, I'll roll for a few; but I got a little dirt devil too that's coming over later.

Me: Alright then. Bet.

[▶ **"Cooped Up/ Return of The Mack" by POST MALONE, MARK MORRISON & SICKICK**] I rode off to get a fresh cut, then went back to the crib to shower and get dressed. Tonight, it was black-and-white Jordans 11's, a white tee, and black shorts—something light. I left the house about two hours later. Mally called and told me he was also leaving out. We both pulled up around the same time. I got out of the car and met Mally at his car.

"You hoeing tonight, I see. Got your hoochie daddy shorts on. Shake what ya mama gave ya, my boy," Mally said.

"Shut up, fool." I laughed. "Your shorts are just as short as mine."

"Nah, baby boy, mine is even shorter. I'm showing off the dick print tonight and these luscious legs," he said, batting his eyes.

"Nigga you a real clown." I laughed.

He adjusted his balls, slapped his hands together, and said, "Let's do this." [▶ "2 Reasons" by TREY SONGZ & TI]

We walked in, and it was a skating rink. We walked right past the skates and headed to the bar. While waiting to get a drink before scoping the place out, Brit glided over next to me on her skates. Honestly, while married, I never looked at Brit as someone I would mess with again. At work, we were just friends. We may have a joke or two, but other than that, she went her way, and I went mine. Shit, she didn't even invite me to her party—that's how out of touch we were now. However, tonight, she looked fine as fuck. She had on these little shorts that damn near had all her ass cheeks out, a shirt that hung off her shoulder showing her bra strap, knee-high rainbow socks, and black skates.

"Sean?Oh my God, what made you come to my party?" She asked

"A divorce," Mally coughed out.

"Facts," Brit pointed to Mal as she sipped her drink. "I told Mack to tell you, but I didn't think you would show up. Didn't he tell you it was an 80s-themed party?" She smiled, looked me in the eye, and rubbed her hand on my back. I knew she was already lit by the way she kept trying to catch the straw in her drink with her mouth.

"Nope, not at all," I replied.

"We are the supreme team; we don't do the themes," Mally added.

"Okay, bars!" She laughed and stirred her drink with her straw. "Well, the food is over there, drinks are here, as you know, and well, come out to the floor and skate when you're ready." She winked and skated off.

"Well, it didn't take that long to arrest that pussy again," Mally suggested.

"You think I got it?"

"Fuck yeah, it's in the bag. Now let's go shopping for me." [▶ **"I'm Sayin" by OMARION**]

We grabbed our drinks and headed over to the food. After getting a plate, we sat down while debating whether we should skate or not. Half of the damn truck yard was in there. I could only imagine what would get back to Tiera if anything happened between me and Brit. Then, for about half an hour, Mally and I were sitting there, scoping the place for who he wanted to bag. I felt Brit eye-fucking me the whole time, but she didn't come over. She eventually came back with a friend, and they sat with us for a while. We talked, laughed, and drank for about an hour. Brit's friend got Mally to get skates, and they headed out to the floor together, leaving me and Brit to do some catching up. We talked about Twin passing, being a parent of twins, my baby mama, and the upcoming divorce, and reminisced on some of the wild things we used to do. It felt good to really talk to someone about everything that had been going on. Without Twin here with me and my wife leaving, it had just been one heavy load.

"Damn. Birthday girl, when you gone come back out there?" Mack spoke up and said as he gave me a handshake.

"I'm coming now."

"Ard, I'm waiting," Mack said, giving her a wink before he skated back to the floor.

Brit turned back toward me, rolled her eyes, and said,

"So, how about I go get us a shot, and you go get some skates so we can hit the floor?" Brit stretched her arms across the table and rubbed her hands on top of mine.

"I guess you better get back out there. Don't keep my man waiting." I said jokingly, and she removed her hands from mine.

"Boy, bye. I'm not worried about him."

"Why? You worried about me or something?"

She bit her lip and softly said, "Maybe." [▶ **"Good Kisser" by USHER**]

"What was that?" I put my hand to my ear. "Say it louder for Mack in the back."

"Go get your skates, man. I'll meet you at the bar."

We got up and parted ways. While getting my skates, I ran into Tam, Tiff's sister, who had hooked me up with Brit in the first place. When she saw me, she was stunned.

"Wait, wait, wait a minute now..." All I could do was laugh. She pointed at me, pointed to where Brit was, and then covered her mouth. "Again? You know what? Let me stay out of grown folk's business," she laughed and hugged me. I hadn't seen her since Twin's funeral.

After we got our skates, we walked over to the bar, took shots with the birthday girl, and then hit the floor—literally. As soon as Tam skated out, she fell, taking Brit and me with her.

Once out there, I had to show off my moves. I could skate very well. Back in the day, Twin always wanted to go skating with her friends on teen night, and our mom would only let her go if I went with her. So, being the good brother that I was, Twin did my homework, and I went with her skating. Being back on the skating floor brought back a lot of good memories. [▶ **"Post To Be" by OMARION**]

I kept getting these evil stares from people because Brit was all up on me on the floor. For some songs, she held my hand; for others, she grinded on me. It felt like teen night, just with grown-ups and alcohol. Mack wasn't feeling the vibes between me and Brit. When the DJ played "It's Yours" by J. Holiday and Brit started singing it to me and slow skating with me, he just stopped skating altogether. I never knew he was so into her. Oh well, it didn't ruin my night. She was the birthday girl, and tonight was about what she wanted. I guess she didn't want him.

[▶ "Yours" by J. HOLIDAY]

Mally claimed he had a jawn coming over to his house tonight, but she must've been pissed off waiting for him because he'd been skating around and throwing back shots with Brit's friend all night. I hadn't had this much fun in a long time. We were back and forth, from the bar to the floor, from the floor to the bar, the whole night. Everybody at that party was fucked up.

"I'm about to head out. Do you want me to drive your drunk ass home?" Tam asked Brit.

"No, I'm good, boo. This guy is going to drive me home," Brit said as she stood behind me and put her arms around my waist.

[▶ "Privacy" by CHRIS BROWN]

The next morning, I woke up with an awful headache. I could barely open my eyes, and for some reason, the sun was shining through the windows so brightly, making it even worse. I didn't remember getting home, but a lot went on when I got here. I stretched my arms, then rubbed my hands down Brit's back as she slept on my chest. I never would've thought in a million years that I would be in this situation again. It was that old thing I needed to get my mind off Tiera and get back in the game. She still had that same energy she had in her 20s. Brit was wild, I tell you.

Let me go back to sleep, just in case she gets up and wants to go at it again, I thought. I got all comfortable, ready to fall back asleep, and then I heard the sound of my room door opening. I looked out the corner of my eye, and as my door opened wider and wider, I couldn't help but think, *Where are my drawers?!* I wasn't trying to fight a robber naked. I was ready to jump up, but to my surprise, it was Tiera. I jumped up anyway, waking Brit up. I could've shit on myself, I was so shook. Hell, this was worse than a robbery. We were both ass naked. Brit looked at me, then over to the door. She softly said, "Oh shit," looking as if she had a hangover. She grabbed the covers, put them over her, and slid off me as Tiera stood there, just watching in shock before she shook her head and walked out. I swear it felt like slow motion. It was the longest 45 seconds of my life. I grabbed my pants off the floor and ran after her down the hall, calling her name.

"TIERA!" She stormed down the hallway and then down the stairs. I called her name over and over. She walked through the living room, and I grabbed her hand as she opened the door.

"What the fuck, TIER—"

Before I could get her whole name out, she snatched her hand away from me and said, "Out of everyone that you could've slept with, you slept with *her*. Why her, Sean?" she said so calmly and disappointed. "HAVE YOU BEEN SLEEPING WITH HER THE WHOLE TIME?" she yelled. "Telling me 'Oh, bae, you don't have nothing to worry about; we're just friends?'" she mocked in a deep voice.

"First off, we're not just gonna skip past the part where you're breaking into my house now."

"I didn't break in. I have a key that Twin gave me," she yelled.

"A key that I didn't give you or authorize you to use. What the fuck, Tiera? You can't just pop up at my house. I don't do that shit to you and I used to live there. That's some crazy shit."

"I'm crazy now?" She shook her head. "Okay... But you're deflecting from everything that I just said and asked you."

She looked at me, confused, wanting me to say something, but I just didn't know what to say. On one hand, I felt like, hey, she's trying to divorce me; she's got her little boyfriend around my kids and shit, well, hey, you get what you get when you go looking for it. On the other hand, it was like watching my heart break in front of me because I knew she was hurt.

"Fine, Sean," she said calmly, shaking her head in acceptance of what had become of the whole situation. She took the house key off her key ring and put it in my hand. "I hope she was worth it." She turned and walked out the door. I walked outside, yelling.

"Worth what, Tiera? You have a whole boyfriend that's been around my kids. Don't think I forgot about that. Why did you come here? Sneaking up in my house like the Ghost of Christmas Past!" I yelled to her as she walked down the street to her car. She got to her car, opened the door, and yelled back before she got in.

"For clarity, Sean!"

"Clarity, Tiera? *Really*? It wasn't clear to you when you served me divorce papers 10 months ago? Shit wasn't clear then, huh? Because to me, it seemed like you had crystal clear vision."

"I wanted to know where we stand, and I got my answer." She shrugged, got in her car, and pulled off. [▶ **"Love Again" by DANIEL CAESAR & BRANDY**] As I stood there on my steps, watching her pass me, Mrs. Brown came walking down the street.

"I got clear vision, too," she said, pointing at my package. I covered myself with my hands.

"Good morning to you too, Mrs. B."

"Good morning, baby." As she continued walking up the street, she yelled, "She'll be back for some more of that, trust me."

Back inside, I sat on the sofa, completely confused about everything that had just happened. About five minutes later, Brit came downstairs dressed in her 80s skating outfit from last night, swinging her keys. As soon as she reached the bottom of the steps, we burst out laughing at her outfit.

"It was cute last night," she said as she came to sit next to me.

"So, I called a cab and I'mma head out before any other baby mamas pop up," she said.

"Yo, I'm sorry. She never pops up at my house and lets herself in like that."

She laughed and said, "Don't apologize. I had a great time last night; you really made my birthday special. Messy, but special. I'mma get fired, but special." She laughed again. "The fact that you even came to my party was a gift in itself." She kissed my cheek and looked at her phone. "My ride's here, but let me just tell you this one thing: last night, when we were talking about Tiera at the table, you told me she moved on and didn't think she loved you anymore. Pulling something like this means she still cares a lot about you. Talk to her. Hey, you never know." She patted my leg.

I got up to walk her out. We hugged, and I watched her get into her cab before closing the door. Man, I need my sister in times like these. Why do I keep fucking up, Twin? I asked out loud, looking up to the ceiling as if she could hear me.

"She doesn't know, and neither do I."

I jumped and turned around, scared for my life. Then I saw Tam walking down the steps. I didn't know she was even here.

"What in the hell, Tam? You scared the shit out of me!" I held my chest. "What are you doing here, girl?" I asked.

"Well, someone had to drive the drunk ass's home. After I saw that both of you were in no shape or form to drive, I drove us in your car here and let my friend take mine. I watched Netflix in the kid's room while you two were up doing the chilling part all night long, ya freaks."

"All night?" I smiled.

"Ew, yes, all night. I had to put my pods in on loud just to sleep. You're going to have my friend consumed by you all over again." I laughed as she continued. "I just got off the phone with Tiff. I told her what just transpired. She's home right now making breakfast, so come on, get dressed so you can explain everything while we eat. I mean, I was listening, but I want to know in full detail," She demanded as she walked back up the steps. About halfway up the steps, she stopped and asked, "Why did Tiera say you slept with Brit out of all people?"

"Because we all work together."

"Oh yeah, that's right! Oooh, you two *messy.*"

We got to Tiff's place right when the food was done. The timing couldn't have been more perfect—just me and the ladies this morning—Tiff, her girlfriend, and Tam. As soon as I made my plate, it started.

"Now, why in the name of the Lord would you sleep with Brit again, knowing y'all all work at the same damn place, crazy? I understand why you always had Twin stressed out," she asked as she stirred her eggs into her grits.

Smolder, Part 2

Tiera

Knock, knock, knock.

"Coming!" As the door slowly opened, I just pushed my way in. "Well, hello to you too, Tiera." I went straight to the wine cooler and grabbed a bottle.

"Bae, get out here. Tiera's, in the wine cooler!" Cody yelled to the back.

"Yes! I'm here for it! The kids are gone, and now we have gossip. Happy Saturday!" Cody's husband, Ricko, yelled as he entered the living room. "Shit, hold on, let me go get my tree. I'll be right back."

"You want a glass?" I asked Cody.

"Ah, yes, girl," he replied.

I grabbed three glasses and the bottle, went into the living room, and sat down with Cody.

"So, what's the tea, Lady T?" Ricko asked as he sat on the couch, crossed his legs, and started rolling up.

"You had sex with John, didn't you?" Ah, Cody screamed. "Was it good? He does have some big feet."

271

"His name is Jerry, Cody. Yes, we did have sex last night, but—"

"I knew it! You look like you've been fucked. Girl, it's been like a year!" Cody said, and Ricko nodded his head in agreement. "Was it good, girl, or no? Come on, you're dragging it. No, wait—you're drinking, so it was bad? Oh, shit, girl, I'm so sorry."

"Cody shut up. It has not been a year. We've had sex twice before. But this time was different. Jerry never gives me orgasms."

"So, you didn't come?" Ricko asked.

"Oh no, I came. I came so damn hard that I cried."

"Damn," Ricko and Cody said at the same time. "That good, huh?"

"Yes and no. I climaxed at the thought of Sean." [▶ **"Hallucinations" by DVSN**]

"Sean?"

"Yes, I kept seeing his face and remembering his touch the whole time, from beginning to end. I had a few drinks, so I was slightly twisted, but it felt real. It's like I blocked out Jerry completely and imagined Sean. Even when I woke up this morning, I thought I was waking up to Sean, but it was Jerry. I don't even think I felt him inside of me; I just felt the memory of Sean."

"Wow, so you busted a nut off of a thought? *A hallucination?*" Cody probed.

"Girl, that's a skill," Ricko added.

"So, what does this mean? Have you talked to Sean? Do you want to work things out with him?"

"This morning, I did. I fell in love with him all over again."

"From your imaginary fuck?" Ricko added.We all laughed.

"Yes, until I caught him in bed with Brittany Patterson."

Ricko started coughing from the hit he had just taken. "You caught Sean in bed with Brittany? Dock Supervisor? The one he used to mess with before you?" Cody asked.

"Yes."

"Bae, go get another bottle of wine," Cody told Ricko, waving his hand.

"What did he say? Wait…… Cody paused and looked at me sideways. How did you catch him in bed?"

I told Cody and Ricko everything that had happened that morning. They both looked at me in shock.

"So, baby… you broke into this man's house?" Ricko asked.

"I didn't break—"

"No, honey, you did," Cody cut me off.

"So, let me get this straight: You see Sean and his baby mama at the mall; it's the first time you see each other with someone else in public. You go out to eat, get drunk, go home, and have sex with poor little Jerry boy because you're upset Sean was with the baby mama. Not only are you upset, but you miss him, so you envision him and get off, making poor Jerry think he gave you the ride of your life. Then you go break into Sean's house, whom you've been separated from for almost a year now—yes, break in," Cody pointed at me, "thinking you're going to catch him with his baby mama to make you feel better about being with someone else and getting a divorce—a divorce that you really don't want—but that's another story..." He caught his breath. "But instead, you catch him in the bed with his old flame, whom he nine times out of 10 had sex with because he was upset seeing you with someone else. But y'all all work together, so that's the kicker. You're over there crying during sex with one man, thinking about another, and Sean's over there pushing the lady he slept with off of him to run after you," Cody stated.

"Girl, so what are you going to do now?" Ricko asked as Jerry texted me.

Jerry

Today 12:30 PM

Jerry

Hey babe are you ok?

I threw the phone to the other side of the sofa.

"Sean?"

"No, Jerry. I kind of wish it were Sean." I laid on the sofa, pulling the throw blanket over my head.

"Bitch, *kinda*? No, you wholeheartedly wish it was that man," Cody said.

"So, Sean cheated on you because he wasn't getting any from you. Not a good reason to cheat, but hey, it happened. You took him back knowing he did, made it work, got pregnant, and yes, unfortunately, had a miscarriage. So why did you want a divorce after all of that?"

Cody threw a pillow at Ricko. "Fool, because he had a baby on her."

"Fuck, you're right. Shit, a lot is going on here."

"I love Sean, and I still do, obviously. And if he would've never had a baby, we wouldn't be here."

"Is it because you miscarried?" Ricko asked.

"That, and the fact that Sean is a wonderful father and his children mean the world to him. And I knew this child would also mean the same. He wasn't the type to see the kid whenever he saw her. No, he wanted to be there for her. He wanted her to be with him. He wanted joint custody. He wanted to be an active father in her life. Shit, he even wanted a room for her at the house, and I didn't want that. I didn't want my children to have to share their dad. I didn't want to share my husband with his baby mama. I didn't want him doing it for someone outside of our household. I couldn't look at that child because it would always remind me of what he did. Shit, I hated that child if you really want to get real, and it wasn't even her fault. I was so upset one night that she was crying in the middle of the night. Because not only was that supposed to be my children, but she wasn't even mine. So why did I have to be kept up all night? I didn't want to be that way towards her, and I couldn't just tell him, 'I don't want your child here.' That would be unfair to him. So, I removed myself from the marriage. That shit really hurt me. All of it hurt me. All he wanted was to spend time with me, love on me, be with me, and I just kept ignoring him."

"Now, now, wait a damn minute. I'm not going to sit up here and let you blame yourself. *He* cheated on *you*. This is still all his fault. No one made him have sex with that girl. He did that all on his own."

"Is it, though? I left him home for weeks at a time to take care of all the kids by himself. When I was home, I was always too busy with work to be with him. I used to take my laptop to bed with me, and every time he would turn to touch me, I would say 'wait' or 'give me a minute,' and that minute would never come. Did you know that this man would get up with me every time I had to catch an early flight? Take my bags downstairs, make me coffee, pack my snacks, take my bags to the cab, tip the driver, tell them 'Don't drive too fast,' and stay up with me until I told him I was inside the airport. All before he had to be up at 5:30 a.m. to get the kids ready for school, take them to school, go to work, pick them up, feed them, help them with homework, take Lil Sean to baseball practice, back home to get them ready for bed, and do it all over the next day? On top of washing clothes and taking care of all household chores. Our house was always clean, by the way. My husband was holding our household together in my absence. And it's hard, I know now because I'm doing it alone every other week. I don't know how he did it for two and three weeks without me there. That man just wanted me, but I didn't care because I wanted this career so badly that what he wanted didn't matter to me. Yet, I was always his main priority. He didn't complain about anything when it came to doing what he had to do for the family."

"That's what single mothers do all the time," Cody said.

"Cody, you're missing the point. He wasn't single, though," Ricko added.

"Exactly, he wasn't. I was his wife, and I barely helped. I was so focused on my work that I didn't even notice my family." I took my whole glass of wine to the head.

"Damn girl," Ricko said.

"Right. You never really told me how you felt about all of this. Shit, you never told me that Sean was Daddy Poppins out here, and you were the workaholic. See, now I didn't know all this. That changes a lot. Because I was just like, 'fuck him,' if he was just going to do all that to you for no reason, I was all the way rocking with you—which I still am—but damn, girl. Shit, there's always two sides to everything. So, what are you going to do, sis?"

"I want my husband back. Kid and all." [▶ **"I'd Die Without You"** by **P.M. DAWN**]

About C.N. Johnson

C.N. Johnson is a talented urban fiction writer known for her engaging romance narratives that delve into the complexities of relationships. With a vibrant imagination and a genuine passion for creativity, she is dedicated to refining her craft and maximizing her potential as a storyteller.

In 2020, Johnson embarked on her literary journey and made a significant debut with her first novel, *When the Smoke Clears*. This work not only showcased her unique voice but also provided readers with a glimpse of her ability to weave intricate plots and develop relatable characters. Through her writing, Johnson aims to create stories that resonate deeply with her audience, allowing them to see their own experiences reflected in her narratives.

With themes of love and personal growth, she seeks to inspire and connect with her readers, fostering a sense of community through her work.

Also By C.N. Johnson

When life gets hard, the only people you can turn to are your friends and family. Sean is a single father hoping to find the light while coping with the betrayal of a past love and the loss of his mother. Unable to fully connect with the hearts of the countless woman he sleeps with, he continues to make the same mistakes and falls back into the arms of pain. He's trapped in an emotional cycle and unable to break free but will soon come face to face with his worst nightmare and realize that sometimes you have to fully close one door to open another one.

AVAILABLE ON AMAZON.COM!